Volume Two

Also by Mike Allen

Volume Two

Edited by Mike and Anita Allen

Mythic Delirium
BOOKS

mythicdelirium.com

Mythic Delirium: Volume Two

Cover © 2015 by Galen Dara
galendara.com

Cover design © 2015 by Mike and Anita Allen

Mythic Delirium logo design by Tim Mullins

ISBN-10: 0988912457
ISBN-13: 978-0-9889124-5-8

Published by Mythic Delirium Books
mythicdelirium.com

Further copyright information begins on page 160.

Our gratitude goes out to the following who because of their generosity are from now on designated as supporters of Mythic Delirium Books: Saira Ali, Cora Anderson, Anonymous, Patricia M. Cryan, Steve Dempsey, Oz Drummond, Patrick Dugan, Matthew Farrer, C. R. Fowler, Mary J. Lewis, Paul T. Muse, Jr., Shyam Nunley, Finny Pendragon, Kenneth Schneyer, and Delia Sherman.

For Mike B.
and the Berkeley family

Contents

Myths and Delusions:
An Introduction

Mike Allen

It's fashionable, these days, to talk about The Weird.

On the other hand, what The Weird refers to can be a bit nebulous. Does it mean stories ostensibly about the "real" world in which a disquieting difference has intruded? Is it a new euphemism for horror tales that don't conform to commercial tropes? Does it describe works of hallucinatory imagination written with literary ambition?

Whatever your views on The Weird, if you're on a quest for the weird, lowercase, here is a book where you can find it. And likely The Weird as well.

Mythic Delirium is itself a weird project. It began life in 1998 as a do-it-yourself zine devoted to genre-flavored poetry, thus guaranteeing that its pages overflowed with weirdness. For several years, our little journal was a sister magazine to *Weird Tales*, that venerable point of origin for much weird prose. That version, the poetry-only version, was officially retired in 2014 after 30 biannual issues.

By then, the second incarnation of *Mythic Delirium*, as a quarterly digital magazine, was already a year old. (An admittedly weird way of doing things, but why quit while we're ahead?) Since 2006 we've published it under our own imprint, Mythic Delirium Books.

In this way *Mythic Delirium* serves as older and younger sibling to our imprint's flagship publication, *Clockwork Phoenix*. Anita and I see the *Clockwork Phoenix* anthologies as a place to house offbeat stories with a genre bent that would not fit in more conventional publications —stories that stand out for their weirdness in an already strange field.

Though it's smaller in scale than *Clockwork Phoenix*, the new version of *Mythic Delirium* is governed by a similar aesthetic. We continue to publish poetry, with the boundaries of subject matters and styles expanded, and we've added short stories to the mix. If anything, the range of stories we use is even more esoteric than the lineups that *Clockwork Phoenix* showcases.

Anita didn't want to see a print version of *Mythic Delirium* go away, and neither did I. The annual anthologies that result (of which this is the second volume) provide the stage where all these diverse works get to put their best feet forward.

Whether it's a print book or a file downloaded into an e-reader, what you hold in your hand contains all of the stories and poems from the second year of issues of the second incarnation of *Mythic Delirium*: numbers 1.1 to 1.4, from July 2014 to June 2015. (Yes, our numbering system and publication year are also weird.)

Let me take the time here to thank our assistant copy editor, Francesca Forrest, and assistant digital editor, Christina Sng, who are key to our quarterly issues existing at all.

I want to emphasize that we haven't simply taken those four issues and printed them out in book form. Anita, wonderful partner in crime that she is, has disassembled all those issues and reassembled them with an anthologist's vision, forging new thematic alliances and contrasts.

Thus renewed, these stories and poems await you, re-outfitted in new evening wear, their eyes watchful, their sharp smiles polished to a glow. I'm proud to introduce to you each one and share the spell of weirdness that each will eagerly impart.

—Mike Allen, Roanoke, Va., September 2015

The Traveler's Wagon Speaks

Jane Yolen

The road is long, but hope is longer.
My people speak to the purple thrusts
of willowherb in the crackling verges.
Wild ponies follow in my ridged tracks.

The road is long, but laughter longer.
Each performance children howl back
at the puppets, their parents smirking
behind wrinkled, smoke-stained hands.

The road is long, but faith is longer.
The traveler's wife worships at the crossroads,
leaves floral offerings at stone boundaries,
acorns in leaf baskets at the foot of trees.

The road is long but love is longer.
The traveler sings by the fire to his wife.
Their child dreams in his cot of moontide,
mornings, the treasures of the road.

Maybe a Witch Lives There

Jessy Randall

"Maybe a witch lives there," Tanya said, because it was an old-fashioned kind of house, with gingerbread decorations on the porch.

"Or maybe a dirty old man," I said. That made Tanya laugh, which gave me hope that I could still redeem myself after chickening out on the bus.

"You don't even know what a dirty old man is," said Tanya.

"Sure I do," I said. "It's a man who's dirty and smelly and poor." Apparently this wasn't enough, because Tanya laughed. "Also," I continued, in a sort of hoity-toity voice, "It's a man who might try to touch our privates, or kiss us." That made Tanya laugh even harder. She went up on the porch of the house and knocked on the door as if she had a reason to be there. Right away the door opened.

It wasn't a dirty old man. It was only a woman. So that was a relief. She was plump and had gray hair. I guess "plump" isn't the right word, though. She was just fat, and her hair was stringy. "Hello, girls," she said, as though she'd been expecting us. "Come in." She looked up and down the street.

Tanya gave me a smile that said *this is going to be easy as pie.* The woman hadn't even asked us our business or why we were knocking at her door so late in the afternoon. Tanya was going to be able to do anything to her.

Once we were in her living room the woman sat down in a chair and Tanya and I found ourselves sitting down politely on the couch opposite. "I'll get you some tea," she said, "and then you can tell me all about it."

"Tell you all about what?" I said.

Meanwhile Tanya had taken a notebook out of her bag and had a pen in her hand. "First, we'll need your name," she said. Then I got it. It was going to be a survey.

"Oh, my name is much too difficult to pronounce," said the woman, "so you can call me Mrs. B." She went into the kitchen and started opening and closing cupboard doors and banging things about like any normal mother would when guests come over. When she came back out she didn't seem as fat as before. She had a tray with tea things on it and a plate with some dusty chocolates. Her teeth were bad, like poor people's teeth always are. They didn't fit together very well.

"We need your name for the survey," Tanya said.

"No, you don't," said the woman, and there was a little flicker there, something that passed between the woman and Tanya so fast I couldn't catch it. I'm never fast enough with things. Tanya took a piece of chocolate and put it in her pocket when the woman wasn't looking. To show her, I took two pieces and ate both of them right then. I knew I still had to make up for the bus. It's just that the kid started crying. Tanya always keeps going after they cry. I should have just gone along with it instead of pulling the cord.

"Our first question is, how long have you lived here?" I said to the woman through a mouthful of chocolate. It wasn't bad chocolate, actually. I took another piece. We'd never done the survey in a person's house before. We normally did it in parks and things. So I was tailoring the questions to the new situation, which I thought was clever of me and would show Tanya that I could think on my feet. She always acts like she's both prettier and cleverer than me, but I don't see why she should get to be both. There should be at least one area where I can be the best.

"Quite a long time, dear," Mrs. B. replied. "Since before you were born."

"Are you married?" Tanya asked, with her pen in hand.

"Not anymore," said Mrs. B., and let out a tinkly laugh like a much younger woman. Though maybe she wasn't so old. In this light, her hair was only a little bit gray. She waved a hand toward a painting on the wall. "My family," she said. The faces of the husband and children were faded, almost rubbed out. One of the children, a girl, was wearing a blue skirt with a green blouse.

"What a pretty outfit your daughter is wearing," said Tanya, smirking. I knew she was remembering the time we made Suzy cry at school for wearing blue with green. Everyone knows those colors clash. "How old is she now?"

"Oh, who knows," said Mrs. B. "So what kind of a survey is it?"

"May I use your powder room?" Tanya asked. She handed me the notebook and pen and gave me a significant look. She even tapped the notebook with the pen, hard. Her message was clear: it was my turn now, my chance to even things out for my poor showing at the shop. I flipped to a new page in the notebook.

When I heard the bathroom door close I took a few more chocolates and told Mrs. B. that we were doing a fashion survey. "Clearly, you have a sense of fashion," I said to Mrs. B. (It's always a good idea to butter them up.) "Which magazines do you take?"

"All the usual ones," she answered, looking out the window. "Which ones do you recommend?"

You can't let them get you off track like that. "When was the last time you went shopping," I asked, "and what did you buy?"

"I went to the grocery just the other day," she said, "and got those chocolates and the tea." The kettle still hadn't boiled, so there was no tea yet. "I went to the Pick-N-Pay. They were having a sale."

I scribbled something in the notebook. There hadn't been a Pick-N-Pay in town since I was very small. Mrs. B. was maybe not all there, brain-wise. "No," I said, very friendly and polite, "I meant clothing shopping. When did you last go shopping for clothes? Did you go to a department store, or . . . ?" The idea, with this one, was to give the person all kinds of compliments and then fall out laughing afterward at their awful taste. This woman's taste was perfectly hideous, so I knew her fashion survey would be a great one. Her living room looked like it hadn't changed in forty years.

"I mostly make my own clothes," said Mrs. B., looking down at what she was wearing. I could have sworn it was something brown and drab, a house dress or something, but now that I looked more carefully I saw that it was even better than that, it was some sort of woolen thing, too tight in the hips and too loose in the bust. All different shades of beige. And her shoes! They looked like something a cow would wear. They had those plastic inserts to keep your ankles straight.

"Yes, of course," I said, all professional. Where was Tanya, anyway? What was taking her so long? I wanted her to see how well I was doing without her. I flipped a new page in the notebook and continued scribbling down random bits for the survey: *Pick-N-Pay, Makes them herself, Shoes with plastic.* "And where do you buy the fabric you use to make the clothes?"

"I make the fabric, too," said Mrs. B., offering me more candy. "I have a loom in the basement. Would you like to see it?" She looked so hopeful I felt I had to say yes.

"Let me just check on my friend," I said. I knocked on the bathroom door, but there was no answer. "Tanya?"

"I'm sure she's fine." Mrs. B. was right next to me all of a sudden. There was a faint scent of onions and something like cigarette smoke about her. She strode ahead of me in those beige plastic-supported shoes and opened up a door further down the hall.

If I went down into that basement without Tanya no one could ever say that I was second-best. It was quite freeing to realize this. Either Tanya was hiding – and she couldn't possibly claim to be better at the survey if she was hiding – or she was staying in there on purpose and this was a test. I got that excited feeling in my throat. It was a test.

"Tanya, you're going to miss seeing the loom," I called out. "The loom Mrs. B. uses to *make her own fabric* so she can sew her own clothes." This was going to be the best survey yet, and it was going to be mine, all mine. Tanya was only going to be the witness. I fairly stomped down the basement stairs. Mrs. B. was a few steps behind. Well, she was old. Of course it would take her longer. "Is there a light switch?" I asked.

"Yes," said Mrs. B., sounding like she was still at the top of the stairs. "But it's a bit tricky." Then the door closed and it was dark.

"Mrs. B.?" I called. "Tanya?" I grabbed for the railing, but there was none. Just for a second I was a little bit scared. I put my hand on the wall and tromped back up the stairs and found the switch. It turned on a dim light in a room at the bottom of the stairs. "Is that where the loom is? In that room down there?"

"Yes, dear," said Mrs. B. "I'm just getting some more chocolates."

"Thank you!" I said. They really were very good chocolates. I'd eaten so many I was perhaps getting a stomach-ache.

I went back down the stairs and into the room with the light. There was no loom in there, or not any kind I recognized. There were some different machines and tools and things, and a three-legged metal stool. There wasn't much to do while I waited. No surprise there, I mean, who goes in basements? Maids, I suppose. To do chores and get supplies and things. I was so bored I looked around for something to point out to Tanya. There was a Bendix washing machine, a really old one, with rust on it. I couldn't find a radio or a telephone or an intercom or anything good. When Tanya finally got down here, she would probably find something fantastically horrible with her first glance, though. There was one machine that looked like a flattener and there was another that looked like a giant porcupine with knitting needles sticking out all over. It made a terrible noise when I turned it on.

After a while, I went back up the stairs and asked Mrs. B. if everything was all right. The door at the top of the stairs seemed to be stuck shut. "I can't see the loom," I said, pushing with my shoulder on the door. "I only see something that looks like it's for ironing, and a knitting needle thing. What is that, anyway?"

"You'll find out!" Mrs. B. answered. "Your friend seems to have disappeared," she said, from the other side of the door.

The stairs had something tacky on them, a thin coat of something like honey. My shoes would probably be ruined, but I didn't mind because it was time for new shoes anyway. I went back down the stairs and into the little room with the machinery in it. I was suddenly feeling a bit tired, so I sat down on the stool and opened up Tanya's notebook. I looked back at the earlier pages to see if Tanya had put some jokes in there or something. Maybe a comment on the chintzy painting.

On her last page she'd written "Bathroom window. Run! See you tomorrow." Had she really gone out the bathroom window? Oh, she was going to just die when she heard what she missed. She would never again be able to claim she was better at the survey than I was. I wished there was some place to lie down, because I felt like taking a nap. The floor was just dirt, so I didn't want to lie on it. But then I lay on it anyway.

Mrs. B. still didn't come down. It occurred to me that if I couldn't get out of the basement Tanya wouldn't know about it until the next day. And she probably wouldn't want to tell anyone where we had been, because that would be end of all our fun. My stomach was really hurting now, and my head, too. I wondered if there was something wrong with the chocolates.

If I went missing for 24 hours, I thought, I would definitely be the winner. Tanya might get some attention for being the last person to see me, but my name is the one that would be splashed all over the papers and spoken in hushed tones at school. I'd be quite famous! There would really be no way for Tanya to compete with that.

And if I were killed, well, that would be even better, because she could never one-up me in that case. Even if Tanya found a way to get herself killed too, she would just seem like a copy-cat.

Oh, good. Mrs. B. was on her way down the stairs now.

The Absence of Words

Swapna Kishore

Music blasts my ears when Mom opens the door. A glance to check that Mom's okay—no bandages anywhere, nothing wrong with her walk, face not particularly tenser than normal—then I put down my overnight bag, kick off my high heels, and stride across to switch off the over-energetic, earsplitting disco music. Things must be worse with Gran if Mom needs such cacophony.

"So, what happened?" I say.

Mom had summoned me by using the "emergency" word and then e-mailed the Delhi-Bangalore-Delhi e-ticket. *Three days, Nisha, that's all I need,* she had said over the phone. *It's a three-day weekend, no, Good Friday morning through to Sunday night? I'll tell you when you come. Please?* Our project didn't "do weekends" as my boss put it—we worked all seven days and late hours at that—but I had been sufficiently alarmed by Mom's desperate-sounding parental pleading. And here I am, tired because I woke up at 2 a.m. to catch the flight. I'm still clueless about the problem.

Mom waves me to the sofa.

"I've bagged a two-year assignment in New York," she says. "Researching and writing on a series of health topics. Prestigious stuff."

"Congrats," I say tentatively. My gaze snaps to Gran's bedroom door.

Mom sighs and plunks on a chair opposite me. There are traces of white at the roots of her hair. Her housecoat is crumpled, smudged with turmeric splotches, and her slipper strap is frayed. She used to be so particular about remaining meticulously groomed even at home. Things change over the years, I guess.

"You've accepted?" I say. I already suspect the summons is related to Gran. Gran's eighty years old, frail but with no known problems other than the one we never talk about. Still I can't imagine Gran living alone, doing stuff like buying groceries, getting gadgets repaired, ordering gas, taking auto-rickshaws to the nearest ATM, and I guess Mom can't imagine it, either.

"I shortlisted some old-age homes where I can pull strings and get bumped up the queue," Mom says. "I contacted a couple." She pushes her bifocals up her nose and tucks back a wayward strand. "One said they don't accept elective mutes. The other wanted a medical certificate and full psychiatrist evaluation."

Fifteen years ago, I'd been away at boarding school when Mom called to inform me of the diagnosis. That someone would choose not to speak creeped me out; for a while I blamed myself for my spat with Gran, even wrote a bunch of letters promising to be a good girl if she started speaking, but Gran never replied. Then I came home and saw the rest of the problem. It still creeps me out, Gran's muteness and the weird stuff around it.

"You could refer them to the psychiatrist you used earlier," I suggest. I can't imagine what any doctor would say now about Gran. How would they even ask her any question?

"Actually, Nisha," Mom smoothens her gown over her knee, "I didn't take her to any doctor at that time."

I gape at her. "But you had told me..." So she had lied fifteen years ago. I feel rage rise in me, sizzling, in my core, branching through me, dividing, narrowing, till I am a network of fire. I force my anger to invert into ice. It turns shard-sharp under my skin, solid as icicles. But my incomplete sentence lies heavy between us.

Red splotches stain her cheek.

"Amma and I had argued," she says. "I'm not sure you remember what had happened the night before you left for school that year. You'd returned late because of some silly friend's party and I'd scolded you."

Of course I remember. 'Scolded' was a mild word for the fury Mom had unleashed on me for a minor teenage mistake, but I'd managed to stay absolutely quiet by freezing in my rage. That time, after Mom stormed out, was probably the only time Gran scolded me. I hadn't known that Gran argued with Mom afterwards.

Mom continues, "So later that night Amma barged into my bedroom all preachy and saintly. Apparently my," she annotates the air with curly quotation marks, "*legacy of anger* would spoil your life." Her chest heaves, her voice is ragged. "I just lost it. I told Amma she had screamed often enough herself. At least I hadn't abandoned my daughter."

"Abandoned?" I repeat.

"I–" Mom's mobile rings. She blinks at the display, clears her throat, and begins speaking in a smooth voice with a cultured BBC accent. Her shoulders straighten, completing her morphing into her competent journalist persona. I wonder whether to head for Gran's door and finish off the obligatory visit, but Mom's call is over and she's glaring at me.

"About Gran's silence," I prompt. "If you think she's not speaking because she's angry with you, have you tried apologizing to her?"

Mom's glare could frizzle anyone normal, but me, I have my ways to meet her crest of rage with my troughs.

"Fine," she says. "*Fine*. One more time won't hurt." She snaps her fingers, like she's saying, *Nisha, heel.* I keep myself cool, distant, visualize my return ticket right down to its Times New Roman font and the airline's logo, and tell myself it is just a few days.

Mom strides towards Gran's room, her housecoat swishing at her ankles. I follow her. An abrupt halt at the door, with me just a step behind. I am aware of the thud in my chest, the clamminess of anticipation on my skin.

Gran's room is still like a world in a time warp. Dust motes thicken the slants of light. Gran is sitting near the window, her wrinkled skin translucent in the morning sun. There are no other sounds, of course, none of the tiny sounds that define us: a throat being cleared, dry hair crackling, the gentle swoosh of breath, the rustle of Gran's starched cotton sari.

Gran looks up at us, sensing us in spite of the absent footsteps.

"I said something fifteen years ago," Mom shouts from the door. "I'm sorry, *okay?* How many times must I say that! You can start talking again, can't you!"

Horns on Mom's head would have matched that tone.

"Your voice doesn't reach her," I remind Mom.

Mom frowns and steps into the room, her footfalls cushioned into nothingness. Whenever I dream of Gran, I imagine her cocooned in a soft grey gel that presses on the skin of anyone approaching her–cold, firm, resistant. No such gel is visible in real life, but even so, Mom takes tiny steps, as if she, too, is forcing her way past some invisible gel.

When Mom is a couple of feet from Gran, she opens her mouth. Her face twists like she is screaming, her mouth keeps opening wide, closing, opening, closing. I hear nothing. I know Mom can't hear herself, either. How the hell does Mom tell Gran *anything*? Food's ready. Geyser water is hot enough for a bath. Do you want this sari starched? Stuff needed to coordinate the minutiae of life.

Mom's expression stiffens. She presses her lips together as if to catch words before they are swallowed. She grabs a notepad, probably kept handy for this purpose. She scribbles something and holds it in front of Gran, who glances at me, then adjusts her spectacles and squints at the pad. No nod, no shaking her head, no twitch of her face. Her hands remain folded restfully on her lap. I retreat to the living room.

Mom follows me a few moments later, crumpling the note. "Breakfast?"

SPOONS CLANG AGAINST plates, cupboards and drawers are opened and closed with violent bangs. But apparently the noise is an inadequate antidote for Mom, because her eyes are over-bright–this, the woman who has never cried in my presence.

I wish I was far away, safe from whatever is about to tumble out. It is as if we are both standing at the edge of something dark and viscous that we have been avoiding all these years. I wonder if we will finally admit that "elective mute" cannot explain that gobble-all-sound sphere that's been growing around Gran all these years.

Mom gulps hard. She cracks an egg with unnecessary force. Whisk, whisk. Chops onions. Whisk, splatter, mop, curse. A pat of butter sizzles in the pan. In goes the omelet mix, and then Mom finally looks at me. "She walked out on me again that time."

The toaster belches out toast charred at the edges. I place it on a plate. I absorb the words. *Walked out. Again.*

"After I dropped you off at the railway station the next morning, Amma wasn't there and her clothes were missing. She had left a two-line note saying I shouldn't worry. I didn't tell you because you'd get tense. You were so fond of her." Jealousy tinges Mom's voice in spite of the stretch of years.

I run my finger across the rough, burned edge of the toast, stare at the charcoal on my fingers. "Then?"

"I called up friends and relatives acting casual and probed them without explaining why. No one mentioned Amma. I wondered whether to report her as missing, but she'd said, *Don't worry.* A week later, she rang the doorbell and marched to her room with her bags. That's when it started, her refusal to talk and the . . . rest of it."

I wonder how it must have been, that week of uncertainty, then Gran returning, and Mom not getting any explanation or even the satisfaction of a good slinging match. I wonder how it must have been, sensing that zone of silence and fearing showing it to a doctor. That summer, when I'd come home for vacations and noticed how sound got deadened when I approached Gran, I'd felt so frightened I'd pretended there was no problem. Back then the sound-soaking shroud extended a foot around her; now it fills her room.

"Bloody-minded, that's what she is," Mom murmurs.

I am about to ask whether bloody-mindedness explained the gobbled words when I remember something else. "You said she'd walked out before."

Mom hesitates.

"Tell me," I say. "I'm old enough to know family secrets."

"Fair enough." Mom nods. "When I was a child, your Grandpa and Gran had a major fight." She sips her coffee. "She stalked off to an ashram at Rishikesh. Everyone was upset with her. Women aren't supposed to abandon a husband and daughter for spiritual practice. Besides, no one believed she was religious."

I am careful not to look up as I quarter the omelet and place it over toast, edges aligned. I've seen a couple of photographs of Gran as a young woman, faded sepia photos of a slender woman in a cotton sari with a broad border, a face that was overwhelmed by fiery eyes and a frown. I try to imagine Gran as an impetuous woman leaving a family and boarding a crowded train to the Himalayas, a small cloth jhola on her shoulder as her sole worldly possession. No Internet to get an advance hotel booking, probably no safe hotels for women. No mobile phones, only trunk calls that needed to be booked from post offices, and telegrams that could be sent. Gran arriving in an ashram in the foothills of the snow-covered mountains, shivering in a cotton sari, or perhaps snug and warm in a pashmina shawl.

"Five months later," Mom continues, "your Grandpa got into a legal hassle, and they somehow managed to inform Amma, and she returned. She'd changed. Earlier she would just get angry all the time, but now her moods swung between rage and a fake sort of calm during which she spouted condescending platitudes." Mom pours herself some more coffee. "Once, reprimanding me for something, she blamed our entire family because she had left a critical *siddhi* work midway and her guru would not accept her back."

"You think she's been struck silent because some spiritual *siddhi* accounting system kicked in?" I can't help the sarcastic edge in my voice. "Or are you saying some other guru started her on another *siddhi* in that week she went missing later?"

"Let's stay focused," Mom says, as if I've been the one reminiscing. "The problem I'm facing is finding a place for her when I'm away."

"How does she interact with others? Milkman, car wash man, whoever. What do they think of that, er, stillness around her?"

"She just folds her hands when anyone approaches her and gives that saintly smile. She takes her morning walk on the terrace when people are barely awake. I've not heard her talk to anyone when I'm there." Mom pauses a beat. "As for that penumbra around her, well, people don't come close, and I avoid talking when I'm close to her, so I don't look like a cartoon character opening and closing my mouth soundlessly."

"No risk-taking, eh?" I blurt out. My words sound more caustic than I intended.

I sense the heat of her rage even before her face contorts, and instantly I am ice, I am far away. I don't live here, I don't have to do anything. I only have to survive for two days and then return. She runs the course–the tightening body, the clenched fists, the eyes bulging out just a teeny bit more. I wait for the outpouring. Minutes pass like hours. But she presses her lips tight. I guess she realizes I am older and can walk out.

Finally, I decide to take a risk myself and lower my rigid, distant stance. "I guess we have a–what they call–situation. Now?"

Mom face deflates like a punctured balloon; this is how her rage always dies–like a tornado hitting a black hole.

"I just don't get it, Nisha," she says. "If I leave an alarm clock near her and go away, it rings. I hear it ring. But if I am holding it, even if it is rocking like mad in my hands, there is not even a *chooo* of a sound."

"How does she handle something like, say, a dentist trip?"

Mom squiggles and squirms. "The last trip was almost five years ago. She didn't talk in my presence. The dentist took her in, and she gestured to me to stay out. I have no clue what happened inside, and I couldn't ask the dentist, could I?"

So Mom's been avoiding Gran's checkups. I bite back my comment about health journalists not doing what they preach. Who am I to criticize Mom when I have been avoiding visits?

"But now . . ." Mom mumbles.

We sip our coffees, and then Mom's lips part, her eyes soft-focus on me, like she's got a brain wave.

My stomach cramps. Surely Mom isn't thinking, no, she *can't* think, that Gran should stay with *me*? I'm holed up in an itsy-bitsy one-room barsati in Delhi. Heck, I don't even take Mom there when she visits Delhi for short trips; we do the mother-daughter ritualistic cozying up in a coffee shop, or her hotel, or just talk on the phone.

I want to cut Mom's suggestion off before she makes it. "I think," I say, stalling for time, when the answer flashes upon me, brilliant in its simplicity, "I have an idea."

"What?" Mom's eyebrows arch.

"Ashrams accept inmates, no? And silence is respected as a *sadhana* amongst spiritual seekers. Spin a yarn about her having taken a vow of silence or elective isolation or something."

It takes but a moment for a smile to fill Mom's face and crinkle her eyes, and the wrinkles suddenly transform into a poster for dignified ageing. Then she's calling people, gathering information, invoking favors with her contacts.

I steel myself and step into Gran's room. I break into a run when I cross her threshold, only too aware that I will not be able to enter the sound-deadening zone if I stop to think. Then I am there, standing an arm's width from her. "Hello, Gran, how are you," I say, and my voice is lost in the silence she enforces on me. Gran smiles at me. Nothing in her shows the energy and animation she had when I was much younger. Her fragility intimidates me.

She extends her hand tremulously.

The last time we'd touched was when she hugged me years ago, the night after my minor teenage mistake and Mom's explosion. First Gran had begun scolding me, saying I shouldn't have got so "angry" at Mom, though I'd not said anything to Mom, just stayed silent and kept my eyes lowered, masking my curled-up rage with a docile expression. I'd expected sympathy from Gran for my self-control, even praise, so when she began admonishing me my rage uncurled and erupted at her. I yelled at her how nasty she was, flinging, for good measure, words I'd seen scratched on school desks and in the toilets, hoping to slice through right to her core, slash her. Gran, after a few moments of stunned silence, said, *You want to hurt me, Nishi, have I hurt you so much?*, and she smiled as if she'd got some life-saving insight, and then she hugged me tightly, forgiving, consoling me. That evening, the evening of the last hug I'd accepted from her, was also the last time I'd heard her voice.

Now her frail hand remains extended, but I cannot get myself to even touch her. I stand awkwardly for a couple of minutes and then tiptoe out.

A DULY DEFERENTIAL darshan of the ashram's Swamiji is obligatory before we can leave Gran for her week's experimental stay at the ashram. Gran, Mom, and I wait in the hall, surrounded by scores of devotees including parents and kids. Kids laugh and play and hit one another, embarrassed parents scold them, women chatter, men argue. Noise engulfs us, but Mom and I cannot speak because we are throttled by Gran's proximity. Her sphere has shrunk but not vanished. I find myself missing work–lovely, stressful work, predictable random crises, buzzing with the challenge of office politics.

A baby bawls loud enough to hush the room into silence. The hapless mother cajoles the baby, offers her breast, rattles a colorful jhunjhuna, all to no avail. Kids, really!

Gran stretches her arms out. The mother's eyes blaze with fierce protest; I shrink, embarrassed. But strangely, the woman passes the baby to Gran, who cradles it. It stops wailing, and contemplates Gran with wide-open eyes, beautiful, kohl-lined. Its face squeezes a bit, and I fear a renewed audio output, then fear that the output will be seen but not heard, and how weird that would seem, exposing us as freaks. But what erupts is a gentle burp as its mouth softens into what doting adults consider a smile. A burp that can be heard.

Gran returns the baby to the mother.

Mom walks off and returns within a minute with the ashram manager. "Please come in, madam," he says. I assume Mom's handed in an over-generous donation.

Swamiji is in his eighties, more wrinkled than Gran, with matted locks and sandalwood paste on his forehead, very stereotype. We fold our hands in greeting. For an awkward moment, his disciples seem to expect us to prostrate, something neither Mom nor I are comfortable doing. Gran beams, Swamiji smiles back, the tension breaks, and a disciple grabs the offerings I have assembled—coconuts, flowers, sweets.

"God bless you, children," Swamiji says. "Anger is bad, love is good. Regret paves the way for good actions, but correct action needs love and wisdom."

Yeah, sure. We've driven a hundred kilometers for this unique advice. I move away from Gran so that my voice can be heard.

"My grandmother has not spoken for many years." I gesture at Gran. "Silence surrounds her. We worry about it."

"People choose paths based on their karma." He chuckles. "*Shanti, shanti.*"

I hurry to add, "She was once trying for *siddhis*. We wonder whether—"

"Tranquil minds hear eternity. *Shanti, shanti.*" He nods at his disciples, who herd us aside. The next devotee in the queue proffers flowers and hard cash. We weren't expecting answers, I console myself. We are here to settle Gran in, not play Sherlock Holmes. Besides, our stay in the hall has confirmed that Gran's sound-deadening weirdness affects only Mom and me, so Gran's stay should pose no problems. Gran can pass for a pious lady who has taken the vow of silence, the revered *maun vrat*.

The room allotted to Gran is small but well lit. Gran sits on the bed while Mom unpacks her suitcase into a cupboard. Outside the window is a sprawl of low buildings and geometric gardens. Residents with serene but vacuous expressions weed vegetable patches and teach kids under canopied neem trees. So very idyllic. I shudder.

Mom pulls out a pad and scribbles: *I am going to New York for two years. If you like this place, you can stay here.*

Gran's head snaps up. Mom had only mentioned a week's retreat to her earlier. I feel ashamed of this way to break the news, but I can't fault Mom; I hadn't helped her, either. Gran extends her hand towards Mom, who quickly steps back. She scribbles again: *We will find another place if you don't like this ashram.*

Gran starts neatening the pleats of her sari.

My mobile vibrates. I step outside to take the call: a crisis at work. I calm down my boss, then blow up at a subordinate before instructing him on how to resolve the problem.

By the time I finish, Mom is outside, talking to the ashram manager.

"Your Mataji will be happy here." His reassuring way smacks of practice. "She looks peaceful."

A prominent lump bobs up and down Mom's throat.

"I'm sure she will," I tell the manager, and lead Mom away.

Mom's knuckles are white knobs on the steering wheel and her shoulders are hunched. I'm scared a single wrong word can shatter her. Sounds abound near us–the grunt of gear change, the swish as she swerves the car to avoid potholes, my own heart, thudding loudly. Car horns penetrate our closed windows. But loudest of all is the silence between Mom and me, thick-textured, dark with foreboding.

Later, while clearing up after dinner, Mom scrubs a plate clean with unnecessary vigor. "You must be having a sleep backlog."

I nod and escape to my room upstairs.

I lie awake for a long time. Past midnight, I dash an e-mail to my boss, pleading an emergency. Then I resume staring at the fan overhead and the ominous shadows it casts on the ceiling thanks to the neon street lights outside.

On Sunday, I mall-walk, shopping for gifts. I am clueless about what Gran likes. And Mom's a successful career woman, articulate, energetic, but what sort of books does she like? Does she enjoy clothes, jewelry? Does she party? Which movies does she see? I have stayed safely distant for too many years–after college, I found internships, summer courses, residencies, jobs, anything that kept me away. Not that Mom tried to get closer.

I select a small sandalwood owl for Gran because she often called me 'ullu' as a kid, her affectionate way of saying I was as silly as an owl. For Mom, I buy a Parker pen, a congratulatory gift for the prestigious assignment we haven't talked about.

When I return home, I tell Mom I have rescheduled my ticket for Monday night and will visit Gran before that.

"Tomorrow? I won't be able to come with you. I'm interviewing a doctor for a lead article," Mom says.

"No problem," I say, relieved.

* * *

A SMALL GIRL holding a doll is sitting near Gran. "Dadima, will you play with me?" When the child sees me, her smile wavers and dissolves. It reminds me of my office, of the wariness springing onto the faces of my juniors when I approach. I try to remove the snarl underneath my smile, the tension beneath my skin, but the girl scurries away.

I approach Gran, allowing myself to hope that things will be normal now, but when my footfall is smothered by her, I feel rejected, slapped shut, and the twinge in my chest leaves me breathless for a moment.

Paper does not rustle as I unwrap the owl. My fingers trace the carved wings; hesitant, I hold out my present. Gran cups her palms, and I lower the owl into them. My fingers brush hers. I stiffen, but force myself to relax. It could be the last time I'll be seeing Gran. I can handle it.

Gran grasps my hand; her skin is baby soft, even softer than it used to be long ago, when she hugged me at every pretext, back in those days when I would let her hug me. Why have I hesitated to touch her all these years? My eyes smart. I think of blinking away my tears, but what's wrong if a tear or so meanders down?

"Gran," I say.

Waves of silence absorb my voice, cool like an evening breeze. Not like the brittle ice I use to form my protective guard when yelled at—no, this is a soothing, caressing cool shell. I feel all soft and liquidy inside.

"I've been an ullu all these years." My words are lost as sound, but they make my skin tingle.

Tears stream down Gran's cheek in rivulets, dividing, combining, dividing. Tears drip onto her lap, and some of those tears are mine.

Gran's lips move soundlessly, but the air suddenly has a hint of jasmine, like an offering to gods unknown. A blessing? Perhaps she has been speaking thus for years, words lost to me because of my frigid distance. Perhaps this gift of calming me is what she traded her voice for. Not stubbornness, not hypocrisy or anger, but quiescence—only I had held myself rigid against it.

Maybe Gran didn't know that Mom and I were too busy being bristly and angry, one by yelling, another by freezing.

I snuggle into Gran's lap as if I were a child again.

* * *

MOM CHATTERS CONTINUALLY as she drives me to the airport, churning out tidbits about this person and that, people I don't know or care about, about her new project, about some press coverage she got. I let the words float around me, an alphabet soup devoid of anything meaningful. It is only after she parks at the airport, after we are safe and crowded in the rush of humanity, that she asks, "How is she? Does she speak there?"

"She was very peaceful. Happy."

"Obviously she'd be happy, now that she's away from me." Mom's eyes blaze with a familiar, corrosive rage.

"Mom, please."

"Okay, so I was not the best of daughters. I tried but Amma never…"

The gravel in Mom's voice, that tautness, tenses me against her assault. But even as my defense snaps in place, her voice loses meaning. Her lips move, but all I hear is a gurgle and burble of something rushing at me, searing-hot waves of lava, wave after wave, lapping, foaming. And then the sounds vanish. It's just silence all around me. I wince and jerk back, shocked.

Shock has paled Mom's face, too–she has noticed the absence of her words.

I inhale deeply, unfreezing the tightness inside me, trying not to resist. *Please,* I plead to gods I have never worshipped, *this sort of silence is not my way.*

Mom's face turns rigid, turns soft, her lips quiver.

I wonder whether to risk speaking.

"Mom?" I cannot hear my own voice. I try again, and again, and finally I hear my whisper. Thank the gods, if they exist.

Mom looks sadder than I have ever seen her. "I will book my flight via Delhi so that we can meet."

I nod. "Good."

We continue walking, the brief aberration unacknowledged, my throat clogged with doubts I dare not utter. I soak in every little sound–the swish of my clothes against hers, the drag and creak of my strolley bag rolling behind me. Mom clears her throat every few seconds–just checking, perhaps.

Standing at the entrance of the passengers-only area, Mom's smile is forced, woebegone. Perhaps she dreads returning home, a lonely home even more silent without Gran. I surprise myself by pulling Mom into a hug. She tightens, but then lets her body yield to my contours. Last we hugged was probably when I was five years old.

"Take care," I say.

The Ensouling of Spacecraft

Michele Bannister

Speak data to me. Speak the long sparse song of descent,
dusty discourse, poised on sudden flame;
sing of hope, the cooling 'click' of arrival,
how cocooned eyes unfurl to pick paths in rough terrain.

Speak of your woes. Patient, eking out metre on metre
scuffing skeined tangles of tracks, I ask you in return:
gift me the scrape of fingers in coarse soil. My body
is always the Rover.
I am trained into your reach, feeling out the rock
gazing colourless, my eyes set apart as yours: tilt, twist.

You are different to your sister. Sol by sol, I shrug
each of you onto me, my frame flexed to your posture;
today I can only move as she does. We are fragile;
we take care not to fracture, it would be so easy
for this to be the last time we could talk. Tomorrow
my shoulder will also hurt.

My far-flung colleagues and I care for you both.
We cannot speak eye to eye, or touch you, as once
years ago, we did: you have moved entirely into our minds.
Our arms stretch only as far as yours, yet we hold hands.
We talk for hours each day; we all
are behind our eyes, turn around, image, go forward.
All of us in this body together.

My neighbour asks, when will we go to walk on Mars?
She puzzles me. We wander there, on six wheels
every day.

A Shadow on the Sky

Sunny Moraine

We found her on the third day, spinning whirlwinds around her fingertips.

You must understand that this may or may not have been true; they may or may not have been whirlwinds, and she may or may not have had death in the ichor of her eyes and knitted into her skin, and she may or may not have looked into our hearts, passed judgment, rendered a verdict and delivered our sentence.

She may or may not have done those things, but we know what we saw.

Given that I am the only one who has returned to tell the tale, you will have to make up your own mind whether or not to believe me.

As FOR ME, those three days before, they found me in the coffeehouse and laid two hands on my shoulders, spinning me around so that my cigarette almost fell from between my fingers. I was annoyed and I did not hide it. They didn't care and they did not hide that, either, two large men with stern expressions and very blue eyes. Foreigners, and not military, or at least I was reasonably certain of that. We know military men by now—yes, something specifically about the men. We know them intimately.

I shrugged before they began speaking, my whole aspect carefully crafted disinterest. But then they told me what they were willing to pay.

"You understand there will be a higher price," I said. "No one finds her and escapes unscathed." They nodded, and I shrugged again. Perhaps they wondered why I didn't seem afraid. Here, I will tell you: None of us are afraid of her because we know her and at the same time we do not know her, and we have long since accepted everything she is.

And also we ceased to fear death a very long time ago. This is what fifty years of death from the sky does to you. Yes, half a century; we are locked in place and in time by what has been done to us and they are locked in place and in time by the tools they use to make us die.

I said I would take them to her. I realized later, as we crossed the desert, that I had been waiting to be asked to do it for a long time. I did not believe that she would leave me alive, just as a storm sweeps away everything in its path. I never expected to return. So really, the money was incidental at best. I had no dependents, no children, no husband. I had no one to leave it to. I had no reason to accept it as an inducement to risk my life.

Clearly I had other reasons. They are none of your business. I don't tell everything to everyone.

WE TELL STORIES of her. These are nighttime stories, tales told in the dark, many times to children, because frightened children grow up to not be frightened, or so we say. But not as a threat, not to make them behave. Once we said *go to sleep or I will call your father,* and then we said *go to sleep or I will call the plane,* and then we said nothing because there was nothing left to say, but then there was her and now we tell stories again because she gave them back to us. I will never tell these stories to my children, for as I said, I have none and now likely never will, but it satisfies me that they will be told.

Our queen of the death machines, queen of the desert sands. Queen of piercing sight and hellfire. In a sense she is our patron. In a sense she is nothing like us at all.

They shouldn't want to find her. In a hundred years they have learned nothing.

THEY PERCEIVED THE desert through the night-vision goggles I gave them, old, rubber brittle and flaking away but still functional in the way that all necessary things are made to be. I had my own set, of course, and as we began walking through the dark all of us saw a flat darkness horizontally bisected by a lighter green. And out of that last there were brilliant green lines piercing downward through the air and seeming to penetrate the ground. They shifted, moved, bars of shimmering emerald. They may have been death and they may have merely been eyes that ever watched; long ago we stopped drawing distinctions between the two and longer still we accepted them as a feature of our brave new world.

Is it like this where you come from? I thought but did not ask. *Is your night run through by the light of God?*

The first time I saw those moving beams of green, I felt awe. It was the first awe I had ever felt, and I didn't like the sensation. That time, I tried to take off the goggles, but my mother held them to my face. *You must see,* she hissed into my ear, hand on my trembling shoulder. *You must see and know.*

We stole between them, black shapes rampant on a green field. This is a skill we now all possess, the ones left alive.

At dawn we made our fire and they asked me for my stories. They were paying me well, so I gave them. And I was in a state of expected death, so I decided that someone at least should have a chance of carrying them back. If either of them survived as well.

In the old days she was the daughter of a distant village, I said. Her beauty was legend, and in addition she was full of virtue, kind and honest. She had many suitors but gently rejected them all, and was permitted to do so by her good father, whose standards were just as high as hers.

And then one day the planes came, and there was no more village. Only her, blood-covered and burned, standing in the wreckage.

God spared her for a purpose and when she cried out to Him in her suffering and her rage He reached down His hand and delivered to her a new tongue. So she called to the planes and they answered, transmissions interrupted and programming rewritten, recognizing a new master. The death machines made new death and she drove the aliens from the desert, reclaiming the craters and jagged rocks and dry brush as hers and hers alone, for her heart is the heart of the death machines and no longer has room for any other.

No one writes these stories down. No one needs to. They are no sacred book, no word of God delivered by an angelic voice, but they are ours and we keep them close.

"You have this one now," I said. "Learn what you can. Stories are maps to what is."

Though I don't expect that it will save them. Not that it ever saves any of us. Not from the planes. And now not from her.

* * *

WE HAD HEARD them in the town, that distant buzzing; we always hear it now, though we rarely see. Another story that we tell is one of constant terror, of children living in fear so pervasive and so piercing that it rendered them numb, an entire generation with that part of themselves worn away. They are us and we feel that numbness. We sit on the roofs of our houses and in cafes and we never look up anymore. I don't remember a time without the planes, though I was told yet more stories about those times, like legends from long ago. They were as believable as legends, and even so young, curled against my father's broad chest, I never accepted them as the truth. But I saw the two of them with half their gaze fixed on the sky, never moving, looking for the source of that buzz, the eye from which it came, and I tried not to smile.

Oh, you will never understand. You who sent them to us.

But here in the desert the buzzing is louder, lower, and sometimes we see shifting shadows close to the sun, and then in the dark we see those moving shafts of green light. Their targeting systems are always on, whether or not they are meant to be made imminent use of. The thing, I said to the two, as I told them my stories, is that now we are in *her* land, where her machines fight your machines, and we can never be sure who is watching us. They have many eyes, I said. Hundreds of eyes in one machine. I think of burning angels with many eyes and many wings, stories told to me as a child when I was still afraid of everything. But these machines are possessed of no divinity that we recognize. They are heavenly fire but we are all forever doubtful of their right to pass judgment on us. Not that the right to do any such thing matters. I saw my mother and father judged by the planes. I saw them torn to pieces by a wave of heat and flame, standing in the center of a crowded market, as I turned back to ask them if I could buy a bag of candied dates. I was thirteen years old, a child, but no one can truly be a child here, and I was old enough to know that whatever judgment had fallen on them, it was not justice.

And it made no difference.

I said, God has not saved us. God has not reclaimed His skies. Unless you consider her.

And then, very far above, there was that explosion of fire. The two of them let out cries in unison, awe and fear, as the fire expanded.

I watched impassively. "They are fighting," I said, and pointed. "The fight is over. One of them has died. Her machines have taken one of yours. One less beast of the air."

"How do you know?" They stared at me, their eyes like great moons. "How do you know who won?"

I flashed my teeth. I am a beast, too. "I know."

THE FLAT LANDS became hills all around us. Our water ran low, but I assured them that before long we would encounter a spring, the spring of Hasadat, which I did not translate, because of course they knew only the basics of the language of the land into which they strode. They were weary but they didn't complain and I suppose I gave them a kind of credit for that. But they were also more and more afraid, looking around at the shadows and falls of the hillsides, the jagged crags where parts have fallen away, as if they expected attack to come from them. Though of course no attack that we should fear will come from the ground.

"Why do you want to find her?" I asked that night. It was my turn to demand stories. "What do you hope to gain?"

For a long time they both sat in silence. I didn't care, especially, but if they were to die I had a vague interest in understanding what they thought they were dying for. Even if they didn't believe they would die at all.

"We wanted to see," one of them said finally, simply. He sounded almost surprised, as if he couldn't quite understand it himself, as if he was only now trying to find the words. "We heard so much, we saw the footage everywhere, and then we didn't see the footage anymore. They talk about her as if she was a lie. So we wanted to see."

I nodded. Then I said, "There once was a story of a jackal-headed god who weighed the hearts of all the dead against a feather. If the hearts were heavy, he fed them to a great crocodile and that was the end of them. No Hell. Only oblivion." I cocked my head, my eyes narrowed. I supposed these people were interesting after all, after a fashion. "Do you want to know the weight of your hearts?"

They didn't answer. My own heart was a crocodile's grin and I knew it was heavy enough. We are all born knowing what our ends will be. One does not live under the singing of the planes with a heart lighter than a feather.

* * *

PLODDING INDUCES MEDITATION—and that far into the journey, we no longer walked. We *plodded*. Plod. The English word—I appreciate the way it sounds, like the thing being done. Heavy and ungraceful. Vaguely useless. We plodded along and I thought, *What is money? Why am I taking theirs?* Was it some kind of reflexive action? Does that kind of exchange become second nature? I knew I had other reasons, but they were still mysterious to me.

What kind of creatures are we now? Beasts, acting without thought?

They would not even live long enough to pay me. Surely not. And I would not live long enough to spend their pay even if they did. I laughed to myself; they would perhaps give me the money and then in the seconds between it leaving their hands and entering mine she would judge and feed us to her machines.

Surely they could not escape that fate.

But even we who have lived in two shadows for so long do not understand her. We don't know her thoughts. I could not hope to guess, as if my guesses meant anything at all.

I PRAYED TO her, at last. This feels like a confession, because I was raised to believe it was a sin. A messenger of God, a demon—both of these things are true. But I prayed to her, my forehead in the dust. I did not ask for forgiveness or mercy; I knew she had none of either for any of us. I did not ask for favor, or a sign. I did not ask her to rise up and smite our enemies with hellfire. I did not ask her for anything.

I said what so many before me have said, what was said at the beginning of everything. The one thing that all of us can say without reservation.

Except even that might no longer be true.

I am here.

She cannot be invoked. She does not come when called.

But she came.

THE GREEN LINES expanded and covered the ground. They blinded us all; we swore and pulled off the goggles, but the light was still there, massive, like blows to the brain, and none of us could hide.

Light of God. I laughed and spread my hands, lifted them to the sky. Behind me, *they* were screaming, and I took no particular pleasure in their terror. It was merely a thing that was true and that had to be, that was always going to be so, and now that it was happening I felt a sense of relief.

Listen: I have a secret to tell that is not a secret at all. From the moment we are born and we begin to hear stories of her, from the moment we can understand their meaning, all of us want to be taken by her, a little. As if it were a kind of salvation. As if she had the power to send us to Paradise, though of course our hearts are all far too heavy. It does not matter—she is filled with the wrath of God, and even His wrath is beautiful.

And so she was beautiful.

She stood there, barely a hundred yards from us, her arms raised as if she meant to embrace us. Rags whipped around her body and her head, and through the few gaps that remained in her blinding light I saw—with bizarre clarity—her scarred face, her hollow cheeks, her eyes that burned green hellfire. Her mouth open and singing.

Ayah. A gasp. A gift.

The death machines screamed and descended and came among us.

I saw them, in the few seconds before they seized my heart. They were all shapes and no shape at all. They were like gunmetal-gray birds without eyes, with eyes in their bellies, with eyes all over their skin. Their rotors beat the air into submission. Small ones swarmed. The great ones hovered, jets blasting the sand away. They knocked us to the ground and there was only light.

I glimpsed the people I had brought there, lying a few feet away from me. They looked as if they were already dead, eyes wide and staring, jaws slack. I tried to scream to them. I tried to say, *This is what you wanted. This is what you have done.*

Her hands were on me. I arched into her, laughing as she cut out my heart with her green beams.

AND THERE IS not much else to tell. I never saw the bodies of my companions. They were utterly destroyed, as must be when a heart is too heavy—nothing can remain. The earth must be swept clean, all sign removed. This is to restore a balance, to wash all refuse away, as it was when God sent the flood that bore Nuh and his family into a new world.

This is her work.

As for me, clearly I was not destroyed, which surprised me. Because there is a part of the story that none of us tell. No one has ever returned to tell it. I am the first. I have chosen this, because stories should be told, and I want the world to know her as I know her now. To worship her as I have done. To understand what it will mean when at last she comes for you all.

There was a home for my heavy heart. She made one. She gave me eyes and wings and the sky, and the light. Now I am very high, so high that no one can see me, but I see you. I see so much.

There is hellfire in my hands.

Perhaps it will be today, when she gives the command. Perhaps tomorrow. Perhaps a year from now. But until she does, I and my brothers and sisters will be waiting, circling like vultures, and we will be ready.

You will hear us singing before the end.

Main Sequence

Saira Ali

For Michelle

None of the models fit.
Hammer our eccentricities away,
Discard the evidence trails we blaze,
Astronomers, try to force us into their tidy hypotheses
But we defied them all

I was thought to be a moon
Cold dark in indirected orbit around
You, burning brilliant gamma ray and neutrino core
Dazzled me

A moon can't survive its star's extinction
Drawn down into its gravity well
Knowledge, then, your best last gift
Which nevertheless I would return if…(red shift)

I did not fold follow fall past the
Discontinuity
Heat rising stretching skin tight light seen through closed lids
Is my own therefore I must be a star.

Time and space warp shift twist under around through me
Nullity tangible altering my course yes, but,
Still I burn, traverse the vacuum
Forging and scattering new constellations

Spinning boiling turbulences dancing down my skin
Until that day my fuel is spent and I follow you down
Across that event horizon

The Nightflies

Sheree Renée Thomas

I remember the place
where nightflies sing like stars
their gilded wings reflect
the dark moon's glide
metallic shimmer, rhythmic hum
beat out a windblown pattern
foretell melodic monsoons
and electric rain showers

Always they came in the monsoon nights
the clouds angry and invisible
in the luminous sky, the submerged fields
lit by black lightning, its lingering
sulphuric smell a pheromone
the air heavy with the scent of storms
that do not break
the skies grown dense, exhale anticipation

And suddenly the night air
would be gauze wings, silent
inevitable as desire
how the light
caught the dark gleam of bodies
pale arcs plunging to fire
that brief gossamer blaze
like hearts that love only when burned

Mornings after the storm
my sisters would sweep out
piles of pale wings,
torn and shimmerless . . .

I remember the wet trembling
when we were like nightflies
blind bodies crawling
antlike in desperate circles
flung out in deep space
searching for the flame

The Djinn

Saira Ali

What you humans don't realize is that your kind weren't the only ones who built an empire. Oh no, your Queen's men were neither as Christian nor as rational they claimed. They brought the old beliefs with them, and where there is belief, the fae will follow.

We ignored the first thousand and one Mamluk deaths. It was, after all, a matter for you humans to sort out amongst yourselves. We didn't realize the danger we were in until we found the first of our dead, with rose petals stuffed in his mouth. Your gwyllion and goblins and spriggans and sidhe eventually figured out the roses were unnecessary. For our part we figured out not to shift into human form anymore, not that it stopped them from killing us, but it did slow them down. Some.

I still don't know what your dryads wanted with my desert.

How did I end up on this miserable grey rock? It's not much of a story. I was a general once. I lost a great battle. My ruler's favored son was killed. I was bound to a rug, a beautifully woven ornate carpet, but still, at the end of the day, a rug, and hidden away in a diplomatic missive your Ismail sent to your Disraeli. It was the final insult of my punishment, to be transported across the world by humans.

I am not ungrateful that the Summer Queen unbound me from that cursed rug.

For the first hundred years, I served loyally, brokering truce between our peoples. I arranged marriages between ghuls and barrow wights, marids and selkies. I hosted envoys from my homeland, taught them the language of the fair folk, guided them past piski traps. I sent every one of them home with a letter begging permission to return. Something we all have in common, regardless of race, is a long memory.

No one warned me that Britannia was so cold. And damp. I followed a nymph into her lake once. Of course, it put out my fire. I should have seen that coming. Four wretched freezing days it took to dry out enough for me to rekindle.

I took a lover in time. She changed her glamour for me, wreathed herself in insubstantial flame, wore a cascade of curls the color of the sea under a new moon. In time, she bore me daughters. I hoped they would choose to travel to my homeland, perhaps plead my case at court, or at least, bring back tidings of my shield brothers. Instead, they wear their hair the color of fresh honey mead and pinch their noses to tiny points. Their glamour can't touch the fire behind their eyes, but they keep it banked.

I cannot grant you a wish, but I will make a bargain with you. Wealth, power, women or men, unimaginable luxury, if you do this one thing for me. Go east and find the ruler of my people. Bind him to this lamp, and wish an end to my exile.

Keeper of the Wave

Jamie Killen

The first time Lena set foot in Pilgrimage, she understood little of the pleasures that could be bought in the town on the edge of the world. She caught glimpses of the beautiful men and women on the shaded verandas above the spice market, but did not know that they were courtesans from as far away as the Southern Kingdoms and the Island of the Moon. Acrid smoke drifted through curtained doorways, but she did not recognize the odor as opium. She saw a warehouse stacked to the ceiling with bottles of ruby-colored liquid, but she did not know that it was wine so rich and vivid that one sip could move a man to tears. There were other things Lena didn't see until years later, alleys full of charmmakers and bird traders and shops that sold only bones.

On that first visit, all Lena understood was that Pilgrimage meant color, and crowds, and the Wave. She clung to her mother's hand and twisted her head this way and that, drinking in the strange faces and the stink and the blended sound of all the world's languages speaking at once. She tried to see the horizon, but clustered rooftop gardens stood in the way. "When will we see the Wave, Mama?" she asked.

Mama squeezed her hand. "We're going there now. We have to do the Pilgrimage first, before Papa and I can do business."

Lena knew that "business" meant the casks of oil from Papa's olive presses. The ceramic pots had filled most of the space in the wagons they'd ridden to Pilgrimage, not even leaving them enough room to sleep. Lena hadn't minded, though, had thought sleeping in blankets around the campfire was much more fun.

"Good," Lena heard Mama say, "the line isn't too long this time."

Lena tore her eyes away from the fruit market and immediately stopped. Mama started to tug her forward, then realized what she was looking at and paused. "I know it's scary, Lena, but it's safe," she said at last. "Come on."

Lena forced her feet to move forward, through the stone arch in the eastern wall and toward the Wave. It was huge, bigger than anything she'd ever seen, so tall that it seemed to meet the sky. The Wave, a frozen arc of water, stretched up over the lip of the cliff on the edge of the town. It did not move, but Lena could see moving shapes within it, fish and larger creatures. Something, maybe a shark, swooped down toward the edge of the cliff and out of sight below. Lena peered to the left and right, but could not see the place where the wall of water ended; the entire coastline was like this, tiny flat land cowering in the Wave's shadow.

Only then did Lena see the line. In the stretch of barren scrubland between the town's walls and the Wave, a tidy column of people waited. At the front of the line sat a house, a cottage much smaller than the one where Lena lived with Mama and Papa. It stood so close to the Wave that Lena wondered if the rear wall touched the solid seawater. As she watched, a young man slipped out of the front door and walked quickly away, covering his face. A woman stepped forward from the front of the line and shut the door behind her.

Lena joined Mama and Papa at the end of the line. Papa turned and bent down on one knee. "Now, Lena, do you remember what you must do once you're inside?"

"Yes. I tell a secret," Lena said.

"That's right. Any secret you like, just as long as it's true." He bit his lip. "And don't be frightened. You'll be safe, I promise."

Lena wasn't frightened, but Papa seemed to be. She nodded, proud that she was being so brave.

'The line moved more quickly than expected, and Lena couldn't get bored while staring at the Wave. They were at the front before she realized it, Papa tugging her forward by her hand. "Go on, Lena. The youngest always goes first. We'll be waiting here."

Lena stepped into the little cottage, heard the door shut behind her. It was dark inside, lit only by an oil lamp in one corner, and she had to stand there blinking for a minute before she could see. Strangely, although the room was dim and cramped, it smelled of cut grass and rainwater. "Come in," a voice said, "sit down."

At the center of the small room a quilt lay spread out on the ground. Toys were scattered across it, threadbare dolls and grubby blocks. On one edge sat a girl, about Lena's size and age. She pointed at the other side of the blanket. "Sit there."

Lena sat gingerly on the edge of the blanket, glancing around the room. There was nothing on the bare brick walls, no bed, no food or chamber pot. "Are you the Keeper?" she asked.

Surprise passed over the girl's features. "Of course. No one else lives here." She leaned forward and reached for a block. "You can play with my toys if you want."

Lena picked up a doll and made it walk toward the block house the Keeper was making. "Do I tell you my secret now?"

"Yes."

Lena hesitated. "Why does everyone have to tell you secrets? I asked Mama, but she didn't know."

The girl didn't look up from her blocks. "You know about the Wave. Secrets are my price."

"Would you really let the Wave come down? If people stopped telling you things?"

The girl smiled, and Lena started to think she didn't seem like a little girl at all. "Are you ready to tell me?"

Lena set aside the doll and cleared her throat, trying to remember all the practice she'd done. "Yes. I have a secret, a big one. I haven't told anyone, I promise."

The girl kept playing with her blocks. "Tell me, then."

This is Lena's secret:

I was playing in my tree with my doll, Lily. I like to play up there because it's high up and quiet and I can be alone. It's on the edge of the grove, so I can listen to the olive pickers sometimes when they don't know I'm there. It's nice, and pretty, and there are birds

One day one of the pickers, Ursula, was working near my tree. I liked Ursula. She was pretty, and she played with me sometimes and brought me a sweet from the fair. She seemed sad that day, so I just stayed quiet and played with Lily. It was almost night-time, and I knew Mama would ring the supper bell soon.

Then I saw Ursula's husband, Rolfe. I didn't like Rolfe, because he was mean and got angry with me and said I was in the way when I wanted to watch the workers press the olives. I don't think Mama and Papa liked him either, but everyone liked Ursula. I don't know why someone nice like her would marry someone mean like Rolfe.

He said, "Ursula!" loud like he was angry. And she dropped her basket, so I think she knew he was angry too.

She asked, "What's wrong?" And then he hit her.

It wasn't like when Mama smacks me on the ear. It was scary, and she fell down. She said, "Please, Rolfe!" but he just yelled. He called her lots of bad names. I know some of them, not all of them. Ursula got up, and he grabbed her arms. He kept asking if she'd done something with someone, asked, "What did you let him do? How many times?" And she kept saying she hadn't done anything, and he kept yelling at her and telling her not to lie. I don't really know what he thought she did, but I don't think she was lying. She was too scared, and she kept crying, and Rolfe kept shaking her. And then she tried to get away, but Rolfe hit her again and she tripped. Her head fell into one of the olive-tree trunks, and then she was quiet and there was blood on her face.

Rolfe stopped yelling when he saw the blood. Then he started crying, and that scared me because I've never seen a man cry. He kept saying, "Ursula! Ursula!" and shaking her arm, but she wouldn't wake up. After a while, Rolfe picked her up and put her over his shoulder and went to the stream at the back of Papa's fields. I didn't see where he went and he never came back. But I think I know where he put Ursula. I went to the stream the next day. People don't usually go there, since there are lots of bushes and trees and there's water closer to the house anyway. But I went there and I found where somebody had buried something big under the bramble bushes, and I could tell because the dirt was all dug up. I knew what that looked like because we buried my kitty when he died, and the ground was like that only not as big.

I go there sometimes now. I take Lily and I sit and talk to Ursula, but I don't think she really hears me.

THE GIRL WATCHED Lena for a long time after she finished telling the story. "Why didn't you tell your Mama and Papa what you saw Rolfe do?"

"Because I knew we were coming to Pilgrimage, and Mama told me I needed a secret to tell to keep the Wave from coming down, and I was frightened because I didn't have any secrets. So I thought I better keep that one." Lena felt tears prickling at her eyes. "I cried after I came back to the house, because I missed Ursula and it made me sad that Rolfe hurt her. But I told Mama it was because I fell down and hurt my elbow, and I could tell she was thinking about something else anyway, so she didn't find out."

The Keeper was quiet for a while longer. Lena couldn't be sure, but she thought the girl seemed cheerful. "You can go," she said after a while. "Remember that this secret is mine now."

Lena started to stand. "Wait," the girl said. She handed Lena one of the worn dolls, one with black hair and green eyes. "Keep this."

Lena smiled. "Thank you!" It wasn't as nice as her other dolls, especially Lily, but she thought it must be special if it came from the Keeper. "Bye!" she said, dashing outside. She wondered why Papa had thought she'd be scared. There'd been nothing bad at all, even though it made her sad to think about Ursula. Part of it had felt good, though, telling someone else about it.

Lena blinked in the sunlight and saw her parents move forward with anxious smiles. "It's your turn, Mama."

Mama started to move toward the door, paused. "Where'd you get that, Lena?"

"The Keeper gave it to me." Lena noticed her parents glance quickly at each other, but they said nothing.

MARYAM STEPPED INTO the cottage and shut the door. It smelled the way she remembered, of cooking oil and onions and dust. The Keeper was different now, though. When Maryam had first come to Pilgrimage, as a child, the Keeper had been a little girl with dolls and wooden horses. Then, when Maryam was approaching adulthood, she'd been a young woman at a loom. Now she sat at a table in the center of the room, one that had never been there before. She wore her hair pinned up like a married woman, peeled potatoes with a small sharp knife. "Hello again, Maryam," she said without looking up. "Sit down, chop one of those onions for me."

Maryam sat, picking up the vegetable knife slowly so her hands wouldn't shake. "Why did you give Lena a doll?"

The Keeper, eyes webbed with small crows' feet, gave her a level stare. "You know other people's secrets are no business of yours."

"I'm sorry, I know." Maryam picked at the papery skin of the onion. "I just…"

"It's a reminder. She and I'll be talking about that secret again one day, when she understands it better." The Keeper dropped the sliced potato into a bowl and pointed at Maryam with a callused forefinger. "And don't you be asking that girl about it. You know the rules."

Maryam lowered her eyes. "Yes, I know. I've been...I've been looking forward to Pilgrimage this year. This secret's been eating at me."

The Keeper smiled thinly. "You always did get more out of it than most. It's nice, not having to coax it out of you." She picked up another potato. "Well, go on then. Tell me."

This is Maryam's secret:

I saw a woman try to seduce my husband. This woman, Ursula, she worked in our olive grove. I'd always thought better of her, and never dreamed she'd do wrong with my husband, even though she's young and beautiful.

But then one day I was walking through the grove, and I saw them talking. I stopped and stayed hidden behind a tree, because right away I could see that they were too close together. My husband looked angry, and she was smiling. He had his hand on her waist, and she was holding it there with her hand. Then I saw her kiss him.

I didn't know what to do. I couldn't believe it, couldn't believe she'd do such a thing. He stepped away, though, thank God for that. He stepped away, and walked off without so much as a glance back, and she just stared after him and covered her mouth and seemed like she was about to cry.

I hated her so much. I don't know if I've ever hated anyone before her.

Part of me thought I should just go and scream at her, frighten her away. But I was already crying, you see, and I didn't want her to see how much she'd hurt me. So I just walked away, into the grove, not even paying attention to where I was going. Before I knew it, I came across some of the men working on the trees. One of them was Rolfe, Ursula's husband. I never liked him, never spoke to him if I could help it. But on that day, angry as I was, I didn't hesitate. I marched right over and told him I needed to speak to him privately. I'm sure he thought I was going to give him the sack for something about work, because I could tell he was worried.

I said to him, "I'll speak plainly. If your wife ever tries to seduce my husband again, I'll have you both out of work for good. Both of you leave now and don't come back, and I won't say a word. If I see her again, I'll tell every woman I know in these parts that your wife isn't to be trusted around their men. I'll see to it that you both starve, I swear it, if you don't put her in line and keep her away from Edward."

I was shaking by the time I finished speaking my piece. Rolfe had gone pale. His mouth was open like a dead fish. He said, "I don't believe you."

So I said, "I saw it with my own two eyes. Ursula kissing my husband, and trying to make him put his hands all over her."

He shook his head, but I could see he knew it was true. After a while, he told me that he and Ursula would be gone first thing. He kept his word. I imagine she got a frightful beating, but I haven't seen either of them since.

MARYAM FINISHED TELLING her story and slicing an onion at the same time. She dumped the handfuls of onion pieces into the wooden bowl and lifted her head to see the Keeper giving her a curious, thin-lipped smile. "That's all," Maryam said.

"A fine secret, Maryam," the Keeper said, let out a contented sigh.

Maryam privately thought that hers must be dull compared to the secrets brought here by princesses and kings. But a warm blush crept up in her cheeks. "Thank you. It did me good, telling you."

MARYAM CAME OUT of the Keeper's cottage smiling. Edward breathed a sigh of relief. There'd been a cloud around her lately, frowns and strange glances in his direction. She'd said nothing was wrong, but he'd known better. Now she seemed lighter, more at ease than he'd seen in a while. She planted a kiss on his lips and nudged him toward the door. "Go on. I want to see the cloth bazaar before sundown."

Edward smiled, squeezed her arm, tried to hide the dread he felt at what lay beyond the door. "Lena's playing under that tree," he said, gesturing. "I'll be out shortly."

The cottage smelled like tobacco smoke and leather, as it always had. "Hello again," the Keeper said. He'd grown older, had flecks of grey in his black hair and beard. He smoked a pipe and stared into the room's little fireplace.

"Hello," Edward replied. He sat in the room's only other chair without being asked. "You've made my wife happy."

The Keeper emptied his pipe into the fireplace, began to refill it from a small pouch around his neck. "She's made herself happy.

Now . . ." He touched a match to the bowl, puffed until it caught. "Let's see if you can match what your wife and daughter have given me today."

THIS IS EDWARD'S SECRET:

I lusted after a woman who is not my wife.

No, it's worse than that. I didn't just want her. I followed her, chased her, tried to seduce her. I even frightened her.

I'm so ashamed.

This woman, Ursula, was one of the pickers in my olive grove. She was good woman, a good worker. I'd wanted her since the first time I saw her. She had beautiful black hair, and green eyes, and her figure was…Well, I'll not go into that.

Please understand, I dearly love my wife. I'd never wish to hurt her. But Ursula…It was like I was under a spell.

I wish I could tell you that she encouraged me, led me on, but it would be a lie. The truth is she wanted no part of it. She caught me staring at her once or twice, and it made her nervous. I could see right away that she didn't share my feelings, was polite but kept me at a distance. It didn't stop me from wanting her, though.

One day, I acted most shamefully, acted in a way that pains me to speak of. I'd been drinking, although I know that's no excuse. It made me bold, made me want to go out to the grove in search of her. She was alone that day, picking olives in a row away from the others. I caught up to her, and said sweet things about her beauty. She laughed and pretended that I was joking, but even drunk I could see that she wanted to get away from me. She started to walk away, but I grabbed her in my arms and kissed her.

She said, "Please, sir, please, we mustn't."

"We won't tell anyone," I say, "It'll just be a tumble, and we'll say nothing of it. I can't stand it, Ursula, you're so beautiful."

I disgusted her. I can admit that now, that the way she grimaced and shuddered broke my heart. She got out of my grasp and turned away. "You've been drinking," she said, walking down a few rows. "Go to your wife, and I'll say nothing of this."

I followed her, grabbed her dress. I had my hands on her waist and tried to move one down to her backside, God help me, but she grabbed my wrist and stopped me. "Stop," she said, and I could see for the first time that she was angry.

Even through the drink, I realized then that I would never have her. I felt such sadness, standing there with my hands around her and close enough to smell her body. "I'm sorry, Ursula," I said.

She smiled, or tried to, but kept her grip on my hand so it couldn't move lower. "It's fine, Sir. Let's stop this now and say no more about it."

I felt like I was going to cry, but I said, "Just…Just one thing. Just one kiss, and I promise I'll walk away and never bother you again." I cringe to think of it now, me begging like some boy who's never lain with a woman.

Ursula kept smiling, falsely, like her teeth were gritted. "Yes, Sir. One kiss, and then you'll be on your way."

She did, then, kiss me. It was short and without feeling and made it worse than if I'd gotten nothing at all. I kept my word, though, let go of her and walked away without saying anything.

I must have frightened her more than I realized, because she and her husband left that night. I don't know where they went, probably to find work in another orchard. It hurt me terribly, finding out she was gone, but I know now that it was for the best. I've been more attentive to my wife and my daughter, and I feel I'm a better man for it.

As Edward finished his story, the Keeper let out a low, happy groan, as though sinking into a warm bath. His eyes rolled back in his head. "Ah, Edward. If you only knew."

Edward frowned. "That's . . . That's my secret."

The Keeper smiled. "And what a secret I've heard today." He glanced at Edward. "You have no idea how dull most of the secrets I hear are. Almost dull enough for me to let the Wave come down, if only for that one moment of excitement. But you . . ."

Edward shook his head, confused. "I just . . . Nothing really happened. I don't . . ."

The Keeper waved an impatient hand. "You don't have to understand. Really, it's better if you don't."

Edward opened his mouth, tried to understand the strange creeping fear filling his stomach. "Go," the Keeper said, closing his eyes. "Go, and remember that this secret is mine. And tell the next person to wait a while before coming in, I want to soak in this."

Edward rose slowly to his feet and shuffled to the door. The last sound he heard before he closed it was a low, gravelly laugh. He stood there for a moment with his hand on the handle. "He says to wait for a bit," Edward mumbled to the woman at the head of the line. She raised her eyebrows but stayed where she was.

Lena and Maryam waited in the shadow of a palm tree. They turned as he approached. "What's wrong?" Maryam asked, smile dimming.

Edward's eyes fell on the doll in Lena's hand, the one the Keeper had given her. He saw the black hair and the green eyes, the simple peasant's dress, and something in him went numb. "The Keeper said he was pleased with what you told him. Both of you," he said, voice faint.

"Oh?" Maryam replied, and it was a poor attempt to sound indifferent. "And did she like yours?"

In the silence that followed, she followed his gaze to Lena's new doll, looked at it carefully for the first time. Her breath caught in her throat.

Edward turned his face up toward the Wave for a long minute. "Come on," he said at last, voice brittle as an old man's. "We have to get to the cloth bazaar."

They walked away from the small cottage beneath the Wave, toward the glittering town at the edge of the world. Lena trailed behind, staring at the growing space between her mother and father where their hands should have been joined.

Deepwater

Valya Dudycz Lupescu

April 22, 2010

Oil gushes like a wound, carrying with it the death of more creatures
than my Gulf has accepted for millennia, but this is massacre not
   sacrifice
offered up to unnamed gods of chaos who live in primordial seas.

As the oil consumes scales, wings, skins, and blood, it sinks like a
   horrible prayer.
I rise to the surface and step with feet the color of moss onto
   beaches covered with corpses.
Where my tears fall, spring up the tiniest flowers made from the
   bones of murdered fish.
When the winds blow through their delicate petals, they chime
   with the sound of tiny hurricanes.

I cradle dead dolphins and scream. Beneath black waters, white
   threads of light swirl
as they ascend, growing brighter until they explode into pure fury
formed into a flying beast of teeth, shell shards, and coral. The old
   god lands beside me.
Our footsteps thunder like war drums as we hunt to drain the waters
   of those responsible
and seal their shriveled souls into shells cast down to the bottom for
   fodder.

I have slept with monsters older than ice; those who swim through
    rock and fire,
creatures of mouth and ash. They will welcome my offering
and maybe get a taste for the world above. Perhaps they will rise to
    swallow cities
before returning to their volcanic dreams.

Eden.Redux

Lynette Mejía

From the dead
Earth, from the sterilized, the cleansed
soil of home I build, reanimate,
infuse and coax the life that feeds
the life that feeds.

No cosmic soup, this:
No mysterious electrical impulse
struck when the primordial iron was hot;
We are invaders, here, my seeds and I,
aliens bent on colonizing, reclaiming
someone else's home for our own.

We come to nourish the new Heaven and the new Earth.
My charges, grown with the gift
of an artificial sun, recreating the spectrum
we left behind.

Still, we're far outside Kansas.
They know,
have always known,
that the light we brought,
(Sol Invictus in exile)
does not measure up,
could not ever measure up.

Ungrounded, they are small, and weak;
corn barely knee height,

beans hanging limp on too-thin limbs,
tomatoes a sickly, tainted green.
They want what I can't give them:
the x-factor of home.

And when they die, as they will,
unnatural endings sprung from unnatural beginnings
I'll try again, shuffling the cards
of variables, planting them
(so carefully)
in the cradle of their mothers' remains.

Earth map

Rose Lemberg

Within the roots, the stones. I once wrote a river into here, inked it in indigo, feathered it in the wind's breath. I walked behind the paths as I created them, afraid how my steps would corrupt their flow Careful to walk only where there was nothing, I pulled even my shadow away from the trees. I inked my forearms in milk only: my name, all the different ways of it, until it dried to nothingness. Brought searingly close to flame the letters on my arms would bake to brown, invisible against my skin once more. Out of the algae-choked pools the frogs croaked in tune to my aloneness, sounds bouncing off my armor of neverborn words. Between me and the world—this world that they said I could not should not make, was unworthy of making; this world they said could not exist. The world my steps marred, the world my breath polluted.

I let myself dissolve in it, sleep, let it be folded between the pages of someone else's memory. For so many years it had gone from me, gifted away sometimes, but mostly just trashed, deleted, the click of the button echoing against my arms like milk.

Oh, oh, not to find that place again, not to find the thousands of places. Burn it, singe it with the skin, scabbed over—it has bled, it has scarred. Let's make a new one. Yes. Let's. You unfold of yourself a hemskirt of a river, black in darkness unlit by fire, and I will let my hair float down into it, and its leaf-laden branches sweep down it rustling: a weeping willow rooted. My words, my body will no longer pollute my world.

And I will braid of your shadows a necklace to string the moon between the cloudsky and the water, I will engrave into the roots your name.

Even in Arcadia

Kristine Ong Muslim

Even in Arcadia, the seas do not hold back
their overflow. The water currents keep you
swimming. The smell of brine taints everything
down to the interstices of your river's upper lip,
that ever-shifting wet line that separates water
from land. You only see Sandra on your riverbank,
Sandra who is a lesser Sandrine, a listless Sandrine
who is a real mermaid and not the factory-made
disheveled one who needs winding up behind the head
so that the fish tail can be spurred to tread water.
Even in Arcadia, the very wrongness of things persists,
the lopsidedness of creatures not yet fully formed
does not subside. But how the insides of lesser creatures
tremble with life, how their ribcages fill with red corals,
electric eels and jellyfish, tube worms summoned
from underwater vents, deep-sea fish with luminescent
dorsal fins, all the graceful, glistening combustibles.

Even in Arcadia, the insomnias leak from the eyes
of strangers. The changelings dwell inside objects
that can transmit light. The freshness of the ordinary
wafts in, grows wild berries in place of roots.
And your thief composes manifold symphonies.
And your messenger casts out seasonal maladies.
And your power cords are safe in the bottom drawer.
And your corpses and starlings rest side by side
under the concrete pavement under the street lights.
Even in Arcadia, the gatherer of detritus,
the pilferer of things past, speaks of nothing
but the grisly charm dangling from your necklace.

The charm, a most unlikely device with no teeth.
The charm, a tip of a deity's horn you claim to have killed
with one blow. He says it is redemption you have been
wearing around your neck. He says nothing really ever heals,
but still you must apologize for what you cannot mend.

Even in Arcadia, Mercury still reigns in his part of the sky
over the two-story house your elders built with their hands.
Inside the house, a phonograph postures as a one-eared sphinx,
conjures with a flick of a needle the menace of a juggernaut.
On the floor and bereft of its rails, a toy train sputters
and wheezes by, for what good are wheels that resist turning.
Outside the house and dancing in a circle are barefoot girls
wearing diaphanous dresses. The girls speak in tongues.
They can float on water. They can wield pestilence.
They can heal the festering holes of the hollow men.
Even in Arcadia, the girls are called witches, diviners,
medicine women, mothers, gardeners of flame trees.
In their cupped palms are golden orbs. They raise
the orbs to the sky, and how their little suns swelter
the reds of sand, the soft splendid yellows of clay,
the rust-colored striations of exposed bedrock.
They raise the golden orbs, and you have daylight.
Daylight streaks in, colors the walls of your house.
Even in Arcadia, the properties of light do not change.
In the front yard, you build a fountain to catch the light.
After a feeble spurt, the fountain now splashes and foams
a million drops of water, a million drops of light.
Then you add a collector of rain, a wind vane, a birdbath.
And everywhere, birds drown and live forever.
And everywhere, wildflowers bloom the darkest of hues.

An Eyewitness Guide to the Sea Shore

Margo Lanagan

It rolls along the promenade.
Some kind of plastic? No? What, then?

It's not going with the wind.
See the safety flags? See the direction people's hair is flapping in?

The colours go over and over, a pinwheeling blur,
like the spinner on the screen when the program's not responding.

People with gelati idly, over their shoulders, watch it pass
—and keep watching, arrested by the steadiness, by the continuing,

by the fact that those who watch only watch;
no one steps forward to stop the thing,

to pick it up, to feel its weight (does it have any?),
to examine it, to find its owner, give it back. They all just let it roll on.

A man sees it in time to step out of its way,
becomes one of the watchers, one of the standers and watchers.

Over and over, bright, glossy, a sun-flash on it, too heavy, too steady
for a beach-ball, and too serious, it draws a streak of silence through
    the crowd,

a curious quietness, a musing one—there's no alarm yet,
just the herd lifting its head, testing the air, keeping its counsel,
      as the stranger passes through.

Hold Back the Waters

Virginia M. Mohlere

The floor falls out from under her. Annabeth sinks into a mile of water, ears popping and chest straining against the crush. Michigan has seeped through a crack in her boundary; although her hands rest flat on the counter in front of the cappuccino machine, she is overwhelmed by the deep dark.

"Step it up, Clausen, you've got a line."

Annabeth blinks at the rim of the stainless steel milk jug. She shakes her head and pours the milk into its waiting mug and ladles foam on top. She focuses; she pulls empty mugs from the right and shoves full ones to the left. She does this until Holy Joe's brief midmorning rush is over. Caught off guard again. The damn water always knows.

"Hey, are you okay?" Jasper touches her arm. "Aw, Annabeth. You are not okay. I'm sorry I snapped at you."

His hands are like a warm bath after cold rain. His voice sounds muted through all the water that surrounds her. His eyes are the green of sunshine through spring leaves, speckled with brown, nothing like the lake.

"I'm all right," Annabeth says, because words are the only defense against falling all over him—a bad idea for a list of reasons starting with: 1. He's her manager.

"Another migraine?"

She nods, hating this stupid lie. Jasper squeezes the pressure point at the base of her right thumb. She wonders whether it helps an actual headache.

"Guess I'll start carrying my umbrella, weather witch," he says, and Annabeth can smile a little at that. "Do you need to go home?"

She takes inventory: pressure is building, but there are no actual storms on the horizon, just the drag of undertow. "I only have an hour left. I'll stick it out."

Of course he sends her back to the kitchen to fold napkins with a towel full of ice perched on her head. The ice feels good, and philosophically she's a fan of water trapped in stasis.

"You should sleep more," Primo says from behind the griddle (one Croak Mister, one grilled cheese). He pokes her ice hat every time he passes and changes the ice without fuss.

"I know it." She breathes down into the ancient Illinois bedrock. The wave is coming; she can't predict what it'll wash up.

The next day, Jasper brings her two more of his miniature jam jars (from the tables at work) filled with weeds or oil, accompanied by pages torn out of notebooks and covered in his square printing. He's studying to be a naturopath.

"You look so tired," he says to her as she struggles to clean the espresso machine.

"It'll pass," she tells him. She'll sometimes drink a cup of Jasper's remedies—if the twigs and flowers don't smell too bad. Her bathroom cabinet is full of them. Mostly she empties a few and returns them every few months. She takes the latest two jars home.

THE DREAMS START that night: pressure, feeling trapped inside the dark. Annabeth wakes night after night swaddled and choked by her covers. The dreams are so cold and the covers so hot.

In the dreams, she's worn out by 1200 cubic miles of water. *Know me*, the lake whispers in the background of her dreams. *Make my bed yours.* She lies to Jasper about why she can't work when the weather changes. The dreams magnify her guilt until Annabeth feels squashed, like a flounder, by her own deceit.

Let go, Bethie, her brother Danny says in the pressure-dream (or worse, the pressure-awake), standing in his Spider-Man bathing suit with a skipping stone in his hand. *Show me how to do it*, he says. He holds out the stone.

Annabeth's chest aches with the desire to take her little brother's hand and help him skip rocks across the Milwaukee Reef, but slow weight squeezes her arm to her side. Danny, her great-grandfather, and the others tug at the place in her heart where the barriers stand. There is no light at depth, only a bitter loneliness that her relatives grasp and haul at like lines. She has to dig her feet in, resist the pull, keep the barriers firm.

When her water family stands in front of her, beckoning, she can see only lake in their eyes. She knows the temptation to which they surrendered. They make it look easy to embrace Michigan, to feed a storm—to let *water* roll through her until she dissolves in it. They make water seem a true kind of home from which she could never be separated, where she will exist as long as the lake does, nearly eternal.

But these are not the family who know her. Not the ones who call her on her birthday, who send boxes of knitted socks and mix CDs with goofy names like "How To Find Mr. Right" that consist of woeful country songs. Even Danny is an unknown quantity now. The shell child from the bottom is the lake's son, not her mother's.

The frigid embrace of deep water clogging her ears makes it difficult to hear anything other than the skitter of her own heart as she struggles at the hands that try to drag her down: family hands with freckles, raised veins, and cold, cold fingers.

Those hands give her the clarity to kick free. The water cannot reproduce how Gran's coconut cake tastes at the end of a barbecue, or the satisfied laziness of Aunt Patty sprawled in a hammock in the sun with a paperback romance novel tented over her face.

Annabeth, tangled in her covers, wonders what her great-grandfather was like when he was alive. She wants to imagine Ryszard as loving and hilarious, with a particular way to mix the potato salad or a talent for the bonfire. She wants to think he would have played bocce with Mother when Mother was a little girl. Annabeth wants to think even she might have known him. They're a long-lived family—if they can stay out of the water.

We're always here, at the bottom, Ryszard calls from the deep. This is the cruelest weapon the lake can throw at her. Michigan is a cold, deep enemy. All of the lakes are vicious. They resent every building, every incursion on their shores.

Michigan seethes. It's a sign of great trust from the family that Annabeth has been given this charge so young. It's a hard thing; the lake's constant, fierce embrace, the struggle every minute to hold the water back. It's harder to know she cannot even trust her own grandfather.

Ryszard let Michigan get him in 1913 in that great, deadly storm. Fewer people might've died if he (along with Cousin Clare up on Superior) hadn't let go. And now Ryszard smiles at Annabeth with eyes the milk-glass-green of Oak Street Beach on a July afternoon.

The cold don't bother you when you embrace it, child, he says in his heavy Polish accent. *The water feels warm—it's the air that stings. You come down, with us. It's family all the time, not just one week a year. Let Michigan have the land.*

Once, in a moment of temptation, Annabeth had said, "Even Danny?"

Grandfather had grinned like a shark; that was the first time Danny had stood beside him, still the three-year-old swept away on a family visit to the Indiana Dunes. Annabeth had been six.

Danny's absence was a crack in Annabeth's dam, where the water could always get in. She wouldn't be a long-timer. But then, Mother was never put on duty at all.

Annabeth weeps her way through deep water, crying the cold freshwater tears of her family. She dreams, heavy as a keel beam, of lying crushed under shipwrecks. Then, always, Michigan diverts its attention. It looks toward the dunes, the vast implacable sky. The lake turns its hate to its conjoined brother Huron, and Annabeth breathes deep, feels her spine uncurl upward into decent posture.

THERE ARE STRETCHES of benediction when Michigan lies quiescent, rolling its own wrecks over and over, water turned in on itself to gentle waves that lap at the shore. When this happens Annabeth exhales all over. She opens all her windows, takes off her shirt, and lies on a folded blanket in the rectangle of sun. High water makes her feel bloated; it's a relief to dry out.

First thing every morning, Annabeth sits quietly. Her mind flies around the border of the lake, from Chicago to Grand Rapids and back around. She slows at Aunt Beata's border with Huron; it's never a weak spot, but Annabeth enjoys the daily reminder that she shares her burdens. On calm days, she thinks of it as "the morning swim," when the water smells cold and clean, the boundary holds firm, and the tug of the waves seems friendly and familiar. It's a pleasure on these days to simply love the water.

Annabeth lives for a little while like a normal person. She goes to work, makes coffee, refills sugar canisters, and unwraps muffins from the bakery. She sasses customers, pockets tips, tells herself very sternly not to flirt with Jasper, even though he stares at her with goo-goo eyes and his dark sandy hair flops over his forehead. No flirting until she's serious.

Sometimes she thinks she *might* be a little serious about Jasper—that since he lives in St. Bran's and plies her with jars of weeds, maybe he wouldn't take off running if he knew about the lake and her family. Or at least, maybe he would come back afterward.

She wanders the long way home from Holy Joe's, midday after the lunch rush or late after closing. She watches her neighbors strolling around and wonders how many of them know they're really under water?

Some do: Annabeth can almost smell it on them, people who could be family, not in the way they look but in the way they carry themselves or watch the air. The Big Tipper at Holy Joe's only comes in at night, only orders coffee, and is patently in love with a spectacularly clueless girl. Mr. Hong at the farmer's market won't sell dumplings to regulars on "bad luck" days. St. Bran's is an eddy where all the strange ones wash up.

Stillness never lasts. Michigan is too angry, and the winds conspire with it to spin up blink-fast storms. October through January is the worst: cold, wind, snow. It's all Annabeth can do to stand up as the lake sloshes back and forth, confine the water to waves gaping up over Lake Shore Drive. Every traffic fatality on such days crushes her.

"Not your fault, Bethie Bee," Aunt Liza says when Annabeth calls Gran's number on the evening after a seven-car wreck. "You can only keep the water back. You can't make them drive safely."

"But if the road had been dry—"

"People die on dry days."

Annabeth cries, hard and ugly, because this is not the comfort she wants. Liza is a rougher woman than Gran. The water hasn't yet softened the edges of Liza Jr.'s drowning. But after a minute, Liza sighs.

"I'm sorry, honey. It's just that your job is big enough without adding to the load. If you try to make it even bigger, you'll crumple."

Annabeth knows this. She can feel the water testing the limits she has put on it, she knows that vast spirit can feel the edges soften in her upset.

"Do you need a break?" Liza asks when the pause has been too long.

Annabeth considers it seriously. Aunts and uncles will step in when they have to. She's not *trapped*. But going off duty is a slippery slope—easier and easier to feel in need of help, if you let that crack form. Water erodes.

"No," she says finally, and she can almost hear Liza's suspicion over the phone line. "But I could maybe stand some help for a few days."

It's a concession. Not a crack.

"That would make me feel better," Aunt Liza says. Also a concession, and Annabeth grins through her snotty nose and tears. Gran might make something of Liza yet.

"Maggie or Ludo?"

Annabeth blows her nose to hide her laugh. This is another concession. Cousin Maggie is only a few years younger than Annabeth, purple-haired and sarcastic, in art school for print-making. She loves Chicago. Uncle Ludo is Michigan's retired keeper and was the previous tenant of Annabeth's apartment. Some corners still smell of old tobacco, and once in a while, one of Ludo's many romantic conquests—in the late stages of dementia—phones, determined to speak to him. He smells of cherry brandy and mothballs, and he holds water back by insulting it into submission. He and Maggie are two of her favorites.

"Ludo snores," she says finally, and Liza laughs.

"I'll call Maggie."

The minute she knows Maggie is on the bus, Annabeth feels better. The deep water pulses loneliness, but she can float above the pressure knowing her family surrounds her.

Maggie steps off the bus and barges in as if she's at home and in charge; Michigan is so shocked that it withdraws into a week of calm, frigid days. Ice builds up over the deep water; at the shore the revetments look like snow forts.

While Annabeth works, Maggie tramps around the Art Institute or sits at Holy Joe's in a ratty tweed armchair sketching patrons all afternoon.

"You're not going to let her mooch free dinner on top of all those cappuccinos, are you?" Jasper asks toward the end of a shift.

Annabeth, who has in fact been planning on a couple of apple and brie paninis, freezes.

Jasper laughs. "You dink. You should see your face! Go eat!"

Annabeth punches him in the arm.

"Hey! Assaulting your manager is not an acceptable form of thanks."

"Scaring me half to death is not an acceptable form of entertainment."

Jasper rolls his eyes at her. She likes him best like this, when he seems like someone who would match Uncle Ludo pun for pun, or whip Gran's butt at dominoes.

Annabeth scores her paninis and little salads. It's early for dinner so they sit by the woodstove; Jasper takes his dinner break with them, three plates crowded on a small round table with a checkerboard painted on its surface.

Jasper is 900 watts of pure charm. He pulls out every story of Annabeth saving the day, like the time a drunk woman brought in her kid and stuck him under a table. Annabeth had spent an hour drawing dinosaurs on order slips on the floor while Social Services and cops rushed in and out. Or when an ice storm knocked out the power for a four-block radius and Annabeth had cobbled together a frightening setup with stock pots and grouped cans of sterno that fed soup to the neighborhood for two days without actually burning the place down. Or the day she'd broken an entire box of plates, one by one. That had not been so much a save, but Jasper makes it so hilarious Maggie weeps with laughter.

"I can't believe you didn't fire me that day," Annabeth says.

Jasper's eyebrows shoot up toward his hairline. "And give up the precious opportunity to hold it over your head forever? Guilt is only slightly less valuable in an employee than punctuality."

Maggie and Annabeth walk out of Holy Joe's arm in arm, still giggling. The night is bitter cold—too dry to snow—and still. A blue ring glows around the moon.

"He's fantastic," Maggie says.

Never lie to family, Annabeth thinks. Lying makes a crack. "Yup," she admits. "Pretty damn."

Maggie laughs again. "Cuz, let me finish art school. Eighteen months and I will be *jumping* at this post. You can take your man and run off to Death Valley or something."

Halfway through Maggie's visit, Michigan rises. It is a windy day in the 20s, grey water slapping up over limestone barriers, balls of ice spitting in the air. Delayed trains. Misery at every bus stop.

Maggie and Annabeth sit on the floor of Annabeth's apartment, cross-legged, knees touching, and deep into themselves to hold back the storm. Together, this is as easy as a calm summer day. Neither of them is taller than 5'5", but they tower over the fury of the lake; their youth and confidence can snuff out the water's power.

That's a myth, and they all know it: Annabeth, Maggie, Michigan. These two women barely past girlhood are temporary dikes, fingers plugging holes, and yet they keep back the storm. After midnight the pressure rises, wind dies, and Maggie and Annabeth sag into their turtlenecks. A couple of mugs of hot chocolate with butterscotch schnapps are in order before they collapse into bed.

By the time Maggie leaves, Annabeth feels human again, rested and strong enough to get through the winter.

IT STAYS COLD. Dirty white wafers of ice layer over one another. The days are so frigid Annabeth's nose hairs freeze on the inhale and thaw on the exhale. The kitchen at Holy Joe's turns out gallons of soups and anything that can be covered in cheese. The lake shivers and seethes.

When Annabeth had first started training, her instinct had been to stand on the stone blocks of the shoreline and wave her arms. Uncle Ludo had said, "You wanna look like a crazy person?" He'd guarded Michigan for twenty-five years. He'd told her about all the various cousins snatched off beaches and piers by rogue waves. And of course she didn't need to be reminded about Danny. "You're strong enough to hold back thirty miles of water. But six feet of it, all reaching for you? Not one of us can stand up to that."

Annabeth would like to tell herself that she's too smart to get complacent. But feeling the lake down inside itself, trapped inside its own vast surface, makes it easy to feel smug. She wanders over to the shore and sneers at the ice. At least she's smart enough to stand back, to keep her head clear and not let the lake see.

Michigan can guess. For generations her family has fought it and its brothers. Michigan never forgets, never stops hating.

ONE AFTERNOON, AS she's slinging lemon scones and peppermint brownies, late afternoon snacks with just a few soup-and-toasted-cheeses for early dinners, she feels a tightening behind her sternum, like adrenaline that doesn't rush so much as fidget in the corner, staring.

Wild water.

The barometers in her sinuses go a little insane—she can feel the back of her face expand and contract. A tall blond man (almond

latte, Joe's Giant Gingersnap) sneezes. Jill's baby Sam starts to cry;
Jill, a regular, pours her chai into a to-go cup and hurries out. Anna-
beth feels the bridge of her nose pinch on the inside, as if it's pulling
her eyes closer together.

Annabeth makes it through her shift, but her anticipation of
wild water grows, so it's difficult to take a proper breath. She brushes
off Jasper's concern before she practically runs home.

Of course the lake had waited—for Maggie to leave, for Anna-
beth to drop her guard. That's how it always is. Michigan waits for
them to be human, and they always are. They can't be anything else.

The solid world is like a mirage, less real than the liquid.

"This is the water," she repeats to herself. It is harder to resist
wild water at the beginning; it's an urge in the corner of her mind to
throw open all the boundaries she has set. Not a destructive urge as
much as an *alive* one, like the first sunny day of spring. It feels excit-
ing, at first—fast heartbeat, panting breath, a sensation like expan-
sion in her chest. She is strong enough to keep back an entire lake.
How powerful would it be to join with the water? Together they
could flood the world. She would become the release valve rather
than the dam. She has to work hard to remember what would come
after that rush of freedom: Michigan rising, dank water filling her
lungs, a cold existence at dark depth with relatives who have had all
the love washed out of them.

Annabeth gets home and locks her door. She sits on her futon
with her eyes closed, phone and lights turned off. Anyone not related
by blood would never know the desperate fight she is waging in her
heart. The water builds. It spreads like a leak through her until she
shudders with the chill. The smack of waves in her head is a drum-
beat of temptation.

"Set me free," the lake whispers. It would be so easy to say yes.
Michigan wants to rise, it imagines itself as carbon-colored waves
that rip Lake Shore Drive to pieces and quiver over the Hancock
building. Annabeth shakes her head at the destruction, and so Mich-
igan shows her the image of a shoreline– white sand, green water, tall
grassland rising into trees. Birds everywhere and tiny, calm waves.
The black forms of gulls bob in the water. Killdeer cry. This image is
beautiful. No more traffic and concrete, no oil puddles in the gutter.
She could live at home in the water and never have to keep the secret
from anyone she might want to tell. Like Jasper.

Michigan draws back; it has no cipher for "Jasper," no rebuttal for warm flesh, jars of chamomile flowers, or white chocolate–espresso muffins straight from the oven on a gloomy day.

Annabeth *will* hold the lake. She'll hold the water back from Holy Joe's, with its burgundy walls that glow in lamplight, its wood-burning stove and board games with missing pieces in a pile on a green bookshelf. She'll hold the water back from Primo. From the Generous Tipper and the painter moms. From the cabbies who always get lost in St. Bran's and all the millions of people who think the far northeast side was swallowed long ago. She will hold it back from Jasper, so he can keep on baking gingersnaps.

The lake withdraws with a creak like wind in icy branches. Annabeth is new to her post, but she is savvy enough not to relax. A tsunami will suck back the sea halfway to the horizon, leaving reefs and fish gasping, before it rushes up and engulfs everything in a roaring gloat and death too quick for drowning.

She breathes, deep and slow, and pulls an afghan over her cold legs.

Michigan regroups. Annabeth can never tell whether time works the normal way in the lake. But when it withdraws, her sense of time lags, as if some of the fizz has gone out of everything.

She sits, and the lake is quiet, just out of hearing. She takes the risk of getting up to pee, to drink some water. After an hour, Annabeth sighs and goes to the kitchen to make some (decaf) tea. She's cold from the inside out, tired more from the vigilance than from Michigan's little tantrum.

Play with me, sissa, Danny says from behind her as she stands over her mug, dunking a teabag. She's caught. She is ungrounded, easy to knock over, unprepared.

I want to play, sissa bee.

It is so damn unfair every time he calls her that. Her heart folds in on itself to hear the name.

"You play too rough, Danny," she says. Michigan laughs through him. Waves crash in that laughter.

It's fun, Bethie. You like to play with me.

Annabeth remembers what it was like to be five years old and have a little brother, pest and object of adoration. Except for summer trips with the family, they spent all their time together, playing mermaid and pirate, explorer, water babies.

"What's in the water, sissa?" he had asked on the day he died. He'd been staring out over the green water, the water that made Annabeth's tummy feel cold.

"Bad things," Annabeth had said. "Things Uncle Ludo keeps away."

"What if they're nice?" Danny had said.

Annabeth looks at the green-tinged eyes of the pale little boy in her kitchen. The years have leached most of the color out of him. "I don't like your games anymore, honey."

Danny's smile spreads slowly across his face. *You would like it, Annabeth, if you'd give it a try.*

The voice coming from his mouth is deep as fathoms, dark and liquid. She thinks that if she stares long enough, it won't just be the lake's voice coming through him—its face will show too. Could anyone look on such a face and not go crazy, not end up like Ryszard, or Danny?

"No," she says, and pushes hard.

Danny's face pinches into rage, and the wild water is all around her, steel grey and foam, cold as metal, stronger than stone. Her body tells her she can't breathe, that water is all around her and there's no air. She tries to remember that she's standing in her kitchen, blocks from the shore. Her lungs strain, and she flaps her arms, struggling against water that isn't there.

Come play, sissa bee, Danny says again.

You'll see how wrong they all are. Now it's Ryszard. *Why protect all those dry things, those shell-less crabs? We're family, child. Not just me and Danny. Michigan, too. The brother lakes. Our water is part of the blood pumping through your heart.*

It's the pull of that water that tempts them all—the water that forms their tears. Ryszard is right. Annabeth keeps her own ancestor caged by holding back Michigan. The lake can't help being what it is, its shores towered over and bulldozed, its marshes clogged by fill and limestone. There are reasons for the lake's hatred.

Suddenly she can breathe, as if she's grown gills. The water feels warm.

Ryszard smiles. Danny claps his hands and laughs.

See how much nicer, Bethie?

She can see: how the water will wash through her, strip her of all her equivocation, her complications. Water will infuse her blood until it's the only thing in her veins, blue tracings turned pale green. She will be eternal, down in the deep, waiting to rise up and reclaim land, or to pull more of her family into the fold.

The water clogs her lungs again at the thought of Maggie gone pale and cruel. Of disappointment shadowing Gran's dark eyes. Of Jasper crying his hot, salt tears.

Michigan's embrace is cold, and its strength flows around her.

It only hurts if you fight, Danny says.

The more she fights, the more it hurts. The wild water wraps around and around her. She can't move or breathe. The world goes black around the edges as she struggles to hold the barriers, to force the water down.

The water tries to sneak around the outside of her barriers, under them, through any cracks. Annabeth strains against the agony of pressure in her chest. No air, miles of water pushing her, but she holds. Her lungs feel shredded and her vision has shrunk to a small point of light, but she keeps the invisible walls standing. While her ears throb with the frantic pounding of her heart, she holds Jasper's smile like a lantern in her mind and stands still under the water. Her standing—her choice—means the strength of her death will hold her barriers for a little while after, long enough for someone to feel it, for one of the cousins to race over.

They'll read her name at the reunion. In praise and not in warning.

Annabeth stands tall and watches that small point of light go out. Water and blood have been rushing in her ears, but now everything is totally quiet and dark. Pain recedes with light and sound.

And then she hears the sigh of a small wave rolling in and sliding back out.

Light and pain flow back all at once, and she drops to the floor, choking up what seems like a swimming pool's worth of water. She coughs and retches until she's too weak to do anything but sit in the pool of cold water and bile, praying that the lake has worn itself out.

Finally she's so cold that she forces herself to crawl to the bathroom and into the tub to sit under a hot shower. She holds the tame water back from her face until her muscles uncramp and she stops shuddering. She lurches into bed still mostly wet, and pulls all the blankets over her. She sleeps hard and without dreams.

* * *

THE MORNING IS bright and still. Annabeth can feel the lake, withdrawn in itself and sulking, in its own way as weak as she is.

The kitchen floor is too revolting to put off—she doesn't even want to try to step over the mess to make coffee. She mops the floor twice, stops for coffee, then mops again. The kitchen reeks of pine cleaner, which is an improvement. Later, she will apologize to Jasper for leaving without explanation. It was another migraine, she'll say, but he'll already know.

Annabeth aches from scalp to sole and knows she'll have to do it all over again sooner than she'd like. She guards Michigan.

The wave rolls out. It will always roll back in.

Visitation of the Oracle at McKain Street

Sheree Renée Thomas

See them l'il girls over there? Pants all tight and they shoes too big?
Walkin' round here, lookin' like lumberjacks. Them l'il girls
don't know nothing about nothing. They laugh
'cause my skirt ain't on straight. They laugh
'cause my lipstick crooked,
blackberry stain all around my mouth,
mascara clumpy, raccoon eyes
like I been stumbling in the dark.
They don't know I ain't got
no mirror no more. They don't know my hand
ain't steady no more, not like it used to.
My aim ain't steady but my vision still clear.
And I see all they see and more again.

I seen the water rise. Me, who come from desert.
I seen the wild and strangeful breed rise
from Abeokuta rock, wailing across the big wata
all the way down
in them burial grounds to 125th Street,
down Beale and Congo Square.
Last night, I sat on the levee and moan
They don't know I seen false prophets rise
centuries ago, ain't nothing new
ain't nothing in ramblin'
I been standing on these corners
sweeping dead ends since time began
since the river I drank from turn to dust
seen them write epistles in piss

carving curses in concrete
pimping pilgrims the pastime of the ages
I seen the newborn choke on milk poisoned
I seen babies struggling against temptations
they ain't yet got teeth for
while you rush by me
frowning at my stink

You don't know
this funk be spiritual
funktified force field

underneath this funk, a shield
frankincense and myrrh
guide lost spirits home

See that girl over there? The one in the fur
knee-high boots, cussin' up storms? Like death,
it's hard to escape the laughter of children.
We will meet again, but she don't know that yet.
You and I will meet again, but you don't believe that yet.

You don't know these mismatch clothes
cover robes that got wings
You don't know this store front I lean to
be the city gate of the restless

Simeon played the fool to mock the world
I play the damned, but you can call me saint
the big black dog guard the crossroads
I cover the dead ends, patron of the misguided
elder of the in between
I cover the ones that ain't got but one option left
But if you can call me by my true name, I just might let you
turn around and try again.

The Nagini's Night Song

Shveta Thakrar

Silver-stained surf my robe
Liquid silk, my tears
Trimmed in foam, so delicate
A maharani's discarded pearls.
I wear them well

How bright, how alien
This sea breathes
My skin, salt and seaweed
Aphrodisiacs from other days
I inhale

Wretched mortal lungs!
Weave my breath
With crashing tides.
O my heart,
Strum your sitar strings,
Call out the moon

Sultry echo, silent song
My sisters' cries, faint,
Forlorn,
Forgotten,
Dissolving now like sand

Good daughters, all
Meek as clams
Twice as tender.

My skin alone stretched too tight
Over this cage
Each bone a steel bar

Crab shells litter lonely shores
So, too, am I cast off,
Remade
Adrift, far from my house of gold
And gems.
Only the stars discern our patterns

A pause between crashes
A pause between breaths
A pause between lives
A single sigh—

I pray the ocean swallow me whole
Drowning is the sea's way to fly

Soon the sun will sweep away shadows
Soon I must flee,
Bearing memories of sleek muscled hips
Interlocking scales
Sensuous serpentine skin

I gulp down grief

Gone, my snake-woman's tail
Once wreathed in starfish and
Sand dollars
Traded away on a whim
For frail mortal feet
Shimmering skylines
A miscreant's faithless heart

Kohl-dark ocean kisses my knees
Salty juices, slick brine

Trickling down my thigh—
Thief! You who steal my breath!—
Who stroke my sari with bold, wet fingers
Who seep, unrepentant
Into my flesh

Bathed in moon, bathed in sea,
What is left but
To dance?

Poor Old Horse

Sonya Taaffe

Here at the end of summer, even the sea
is shedding its leaves, curled letters
come ashore in bottles of float-flawed glass,
a puddle of thick-furred silver
dropped like a towel in the dunes' rambling lee,
girls with gulls' breasts leaning from whitened rocks,
their voices wind-thrown, their arms open wide as sails.
Each ninth wave arches the white necks of drowned horses,
thundering sailors to shore beneath their hooves.
Take the coin from the hand of the last, his black coat
the shale crunching sun-hot beneath your sandy feet:
it will buy you passage
anywhere the sea burns silver with dolphins' backs.
Take your skin from the shade of the beach plums,
your heading from the sirens calling across the buoys.
Leave me a message rolled in an antique map,
its winds and nereids all my winter's study
until spring foam flowers back your face to me.

Time Travel Autumn

Wendy Rathbone

The fields are restless
Old orange Jack comes to life again
The moon's a criminal
  among the orphan trees
Ancient Septembers
New Octobers
Rust eye-shadow
  from old chains
  makes the ghosts cry
The deathclock knows no time
  only spun fall
  ubiquitous forever dust-man
  repeating and repeating
  the same cicada songs
Madness smells of stars
  dragon-hot
Even the bones of the dead
  ache
Autumn
  make me
  a winter sun
  in these crushed
  glass hours
  take me
  mica child
  street god
  to the lost avenues of
  an ebon moon

Love Song

John Philip Johnson

Delicate as the teal of a sunrise
refracted in the mist
of the morning bird's blood
on the far hills of Incaldrion

Delicate as a youth's first
acid wash, the sparkling orange
of fire burning off the layers
to the wet sheen that rests beneath

Delicate as the moonsingers's last note
after all has been sung, trailing off
as though being eaten by the silence,
the air-bleeding, pounding silence

Delicate as the appetite
that wakes at dawn, that takes wing
and gathers itself like a fist
into the fullness of day

As delicately, so delicately,
shall your blood and thoughts enter mine,
before the floods of confusion
and the heartwork of dying,
before we enter the drowning pools
and are engulfed in their utter calm.

Behind Glass

Brady Golden

When the old man is away, it sometimes seems that our eyes might be on the verge of adjusting to the darkness. The black impenetrable wall begins to take on a bit of depth. Hints of shapes come into focus. Then he returns, obliterating our night vision, and it all goes away again. A sphere of light surrounds him. It follows him around the room like a spotlight tracking an actor across a stage, sliding across the hardwood floor. It shifts and churns as though it were casting through murky water.

Sometimes he brings home a stack of children's books from the library, but tonight he reads to us from *The Times*, and the young ones are bored. They stir restlessly. He has only been back for a few minutes, has not even thought to take off his jacket yet, when we feel a brief, gentle vibration, and he stops mid-sentence, mid-word even. We ask what he's heard, but he shushes us. He sits still, head cocked to the side, a finger pressed to his lips. We feel the vibration again. This time we know better than to make a sound. Hesitantly, he rises from his armchair and crosses the apartment. He passes the small table where he deposits his wallet, keys, and a stack of mail each night when he comes home from work. We watch him crack open the door. Whoever stands on the other side is invisible to us. He, she, resists the light.

Yes? The old man's voice is quieter now than when he speaks to us. *Yes, of course. I remember.*

We strain to hear the visitor's words but the voice is so faint, it might as well be coming through a foot of cement. A man? A woman? It's impossible to tell. And are those muffled whimpers and clicks actually words at all? Are they even a language? We whisper and twitch. The young ones shrink away, nervous. Some of us attempt to console them. The rest simply listen. He never gets visitors.

I see, he says. *But if you recall, we did have an agreement—*

The visitor cuts him off.

I understand, believe me. And it's not that I'm unsympathetic—

He stops and waits through another burst of noise.

I'm . . . not sure that's such a good idea.

A flurry of movement, and the old man staggers back. We flinch and gasp. What violence is this? We press forward to help him, but of course, the way is blocked. Uselessly, futilely, we shout and flail. The young ones begin to cry, and there's no one to comfort them this time. He straightens, runs his hands down the front of his shirt, and casts us what's intended as a reassuring glance. We fall still, but it's an alert stillness, anxious, taut. The visitor, in the apartment now, shuts the door and begins to speak again. The words are the same gibber-ish, but the tone, at least, is clear. Pleading. Desperation. For a mo-ment, the figure leans into the circle of light, and we catch a glimpse of long yellow hair, a soft jaw-line, a slender arm, and we realize this visitor is a woman. Then the old man steps back. The light follows him, and she is again cast in darkness.

All right, all right, but just for a moment, he says. *Then you have to go. I must insist. I'm sorry. I must.*

We hiss amongst ourselves. Someone must know this woman, but we saw so little, and for such a short time. And anyway, the memories, our memories, they don't last. No matter why she is here, no matter what she wants, the old man won't let her hurt us. He promised us that. No one would ever hurt us, and we would never be alone again. And we trust him. He has never given us cause not to. At least, we don't think he has. The memories don't last.

He moves toward us and she follows. We think we have a sense of the shape and size of his apartment, but that's self-delusion. All we know is him. Everything else is dark and vague. When he gets close, his face bends and spreads in the glass. Frown lines and crow's-feet cut deep grooves in his face. Patches of white stubble stand out on his chin and cheeks. His skin has a yellow tint. On a certain level, we can tell that he is sick, and yet he contains so much life. To us, he teems with it.

Here she is. Safe and sound. The woman makes a sound that we understand to be a question. *No, nothing to see, but I promise you, she's there.*

Which of us is he talking about? She. That should narrow it down. We realize that we've never bothered to learn one another's sexes, which seems absurd, even negligent. We have all the time in

the world to talk, to gossip, yet we've somehow managed to let this
detail slip. We're unsure if anyone even remembers. Some claim to,
but their voices betray their uncertainty. We try to conjure memo-
ries, any memories that might help us make sense of what's happen-
ing here, but the flashes collide and tumble over each other. A room
with red walls and white-trimmed windows. A little boy with dark
skin and pale, wet eyes. Running through a forested canyon, the trees
awash in orange sunlight, as sweat runs down our face and fast, giddy
rock music blares in our ears. There's no way of knowing to whom
each memory belongs, if they can be said to belong to anyone at all.
Maybe if we could control them, we could parse out some meaning,
but they come too fast, one atop the other. Longing, love, joy, grief,
and whatever else might be floating around in here gets smeared to-
gether like a child's fingerpainting into an aching mess of brown.

A shape rises up before us like some benthic creature drifting
through the ocean. It's a hand, we realize. Her hand, silhouetted in
his lazy, murky light. It's an occultation, the moon blocking out the
sun, and it's coming toward us, slowly, cautiously. We're transfixed
as we begin to understand what she's about to do. We haven't been
touched in so long. Even when the old man cleans the glass, he wears
rubber gloves. We itch with our isolation. We open ourselves up to
the sensation. An instant before her palm reaches the glass, the old
man's own hand darts out and latches onto her.

Please, I must ask you not to disturb them.

He has told us before that just as people are hidden from us, so
are we from them, but he's never managed to explain, or bothered to,
what makes him different. He won't tell us if this ability is something
he learned, was taught, or was born with. He evades the question,
and no one has ever been able to decipher his reluctance. Now, as he
stands before us next to this woman-shaped shadow, peering in at his
collection, we realize there is something else he's never told us: Why.
What does he want with us?

She is speaking now. He listens with his eyes lowered, his lips
drawn tight. When she finishes, he eases a slow, audible breath out
through his nose and waits several seconds before he responds.

*You're forgetting what it was like. The slamming doors? The fur-
niture flying around the room? The mirrors shattering in their frames?
Have you forgotten how afraid you were?* Terrified. *That was the word
you used when you called me. Terrified.*

It takes a moment to figure out that he's talking about us. Or one of us, anyway, and that distinction is meaningless. We remember none of those things, but we can't help but believe them. A cold weight settles within us. The glass begins to vibrate.

I've been doing this for a long time. She's not alone in there. There are thirty-six of them. Thirty-six, just like her. They talk to each other. They keep each other company. They're her family now. And she has me. I take good care of her, just like I promised. I'm a friend to her. She's not alone anymore. The woman begins to speak, but he cuts her off. *Yes, she was. She was alone. You think that because she was in your house, that she was with you, but she was not, any more than you were with her. She has been alone for years. All alone, trying to find you, sensing your presence, calling out to you, but unable to reach you. I know you can imagine what that was like. How agonizing it must have been. How terrifying for* her.

Another pause for the woman's protestations.

Yes, dammit, all alone. All alone since she—

We tense up, crackling and trembling in anticipation of the word, the word that he never says, that no one is ever allowed to say. It doesn't mean what you think. It doesn't mean what it means. It is not what it is. There is a popping sound, and a miniature lightning bolt only a few inches long appears in the glass. The old man flinches and falls silent. We unwind, but only just. He should know better.

He takes the woman by the arm and begins to lead her away. When he speaks again, his voice is more subdued than before. *I can't tell you why your daughter failed to move on, and I can't bring her that peace. But I like to think I've brought her* some *peace, at least. She's safe here with me. She's found a home. For lack of a better word, a life, and she's learned to let go of the one that came before. And now it's time for you to do the same. Find peace. Let go.*

They've reached the door. He opens it, and with a hand on the small of her back, begins to usher her through. Icy panic grips us. The things he is saying, they're not true. We never *found* a home here; we were *brought* here, abducted and dumped into our glass world. And we never *learned to let go;* we *forgot.* Our memories are vaporous things, and our connections to our lives before are fragile. He exploited that fragility, let us forget when it was the last thing in the world we wanted to do. This woman—this mother—*our* mother— we cannot let her leave. We cannot lose her again. We cry out. With a high-pitched shriek, the lightning-bolt crack spreads, zigzagging its way down the front of the glass.

As one, they look to us.

No, wait—

But she's already running toward us, arms outstretched. We surge to her, crashing into each other, until we hit the glass like a train hits a car stalled on the tracks. There is a sharp crack and it falls away. We take flight, we spin, free, uncontained, unconstricted, unwhole, unfocused, lost. We cannot see the woman, but we hear her screams. One word, over and over again. A nonsense word. It has no meaning. A name. Names are for the living, not for us. We look for each other, but there's only noise and movement. We look for him, and we see his light, but there's so much darkness in between. The darkness is minefield. There are so many hard things, and their edges are sharp.

Orpheus

Geoffrey A. Landis

Always, after, he would tell that one tiny lie
so often he would come to believe it himself—

When he walked out of the underworld,
every sense at its pitch,
straining his ears for the sound of her footfalls,
trying to catch her womanly scent,
feeling with the hairs at the back of his neck for the lightest touch
 of her breath

he heard only his own breath
felt only the prickling of his own sweat
smelled only the stink of sulfur seeping from the rocks of the Earth

Telling himself don't look, don't look, don't look, don't look
knowing that a man can only escape from hell once
that if ever he tried to go back,
this time he would be allowed no requests

And the king of hell,
who grants no favors,
who lets none from his kingdom return,
the king who does not laugh
who granted him one favor
who gave him leave to return one from his kingdom to the world
who made him promise just one thing,
to never look behind

And he
kept faith with the king of hell,
for the sake of his love he did not look back
until that final moment,
as he emerged
from the crevice between shattered boulders
emerged from darkness into blinding brightness
and turned back to the shadows—

always, after, he would tell
that he saw her, there,
alive
for one moment
for one moment only
before she slipped away
silent as a dream
silent as shadows—

But blinded by the brightness of the world,
to Orpheus's day-dazzled eyes,
in shadows darker than black:
he saw nothing.

This is the lie Orpheus tells himself:
that when he left the underworld
he was not alone.

Anonymity

Sonya Taaffe

As cutpurses in his good queen's day were branded and false coiners clipped of their ears to noise their shame, there are times when Will has considered suggesting that Kit have tattooed somewhere memorable about his person the legend SOMEONE IS WRONG ON THE INTERNET, but he knows it to be a practice of sufficient provocation it must appeal to that same Marley who praised Lucan before Vergil and once called the presbyter John Christ's bedmate, and then he would have to look at it every night. He has written out instead in his cleanest hand DON'T FEED THE TROLLS and fastened up the paper like a latter-day Luther, with the small brass tacks that glint like his fellow's hair, and observes Marlowe ignore it as studiously, with the same straight-backed self-assurance as looks out of the portrait he swears he did not sit for, except that Will has seen him take the identical stance in arguments, which he loses. He types badly, with quill-callused fingers; he appears at times to be giving his notebook the Agincourt salute. "This cannot go on, Kit—" Will hears himself like a fretting prompter, the players recalcitrant and the papers all foul, though he has as much temper at these small hours of the night as Kit has left coffee in his cup. "Thou'lt come to another reckoning—not greater than Deptford's, I grant thee, but neither so swiftly dispatched. Come to *bed*, mad Kit. It will not end. What profit in it, if Faustus scape Hell's fire to be anatomized upon a pin?" But though he has seen him stage-manage the passions of others with little more than a tousling look and the dare of a word or two, the ironical temper of scholars and kings (and not a little conscious of the part), he never has seen Christofer Marlow of Canterbury and the Admiral's Men stand down from a fight, not with swords in Shoreditch or Cambridge scoffing, and he has besides a green curiosity for the by-trees of foolery that Will cannot stomach any longer to plash or prune himself: the rumors so subterranean they have bottomed out of earth, the secret chains of inheritance with no blood in them, the castles of ramshackle air. By the screen's corpse-casting fox-glim, Marlowe has a ghastlier look than Mephistophilis, but he sounds as tirelessly sardonic: "Throat-cut in Southwark, Will. And by *thy* hand, over a matter of authoring. God's light, if I read another line, I shall have conceived of Jonson and fathered bastards on Tom Nashe."—"And murdered farting Oxford, Kit, I *know*. Have done, for pity," and Kit with his intelligencer's wryness sighs. "They are still wrong, Will, whether I come to bed or no." But he must laugh when he does, because Will is laughing, laying aside his book, a small neat-bearded man, bright-earringed, with nothing much else of the portrait about him: "Ay, Kit. Tomorrow. Thou dost know, they'll not have gotten it then. Nor ever *this*."

Eating and Being Eaten

Jane Yolen

"And she closed her eyes, and imagined what the world would be like if worms were happier once they'd been eaten."
—Teresa Matlock

This is an eating world, the child says, even Chicken Licken,
my great heroine, She Who Offers Warnings, gets eaten.
Probably in a good piccata sauce, her mother muses.

At the table they give thanks for happy vegetables,
though both have read about carrots screaming
 when pulled from the ground.

Missionaries, mother says under her breath, sing prayers
in the cannibals' pot. Though I expect springboks
curse the lion, even in the midst of being devoured.

From her perch in the story book, Chicken Licken
imagines a different, more satisfying world,
one where worms become happier once they're eaten,

having been washed clean and holy in the beak.

All the Tribes of the Earth
Shall Mourn

Nathaniel Lee

"Angels!"

Peary nearly got trampled when the cry went up down the street. Trust him to be walking on a crowded sidewalk when there was a visitation. The mob rushed past, and Peary fought his way against the current like an exhausted swimmer battling a riptide. At last, he reached the sheltered shoal of a shop display window, where a next-generation plasma-high-whatever television was showing the news. Peary tasted copper, touched his lip and found it bleeding. Someone's stray elbow, most likely. He leaned against the glass, cold and hard and fragile at his back. A block away, the crowds were massing around a focal point, hands held high, fingers straining and groping to touch their heavenly visitor. A babble of voices cried out all at once; from this distance, Peary could only make out an occasional "heal me!" or "bless me!" There was an awful lot of "me" whenever angels showed up.

Peary raised a hand to shade his eyes from the glaring cotton-ball whiteness of the wintery sky. The multitude of arms were all reaching toward something he couldn't quite make out, something small and pale, like a handful of snow. Peary wondered what everyone else saw. He tugged a handkerchief out of his back pocket and dabbed at his lip, waiting for the bleeding to slow. From the screen at his back, he could just make out the muffled sound of the news anchor, who was doing the day's roundup of angel news. Peary smiled; if that wasn't serendipity, what was? Angels were barely news anymore, but like a war or a long-running celebrity trial, the news programs seemed to feel obligated to mention them periodically.

Peary hitched himself to the side to avoid the continuing flow of would-be supplicants, slowed now from a rush to a trickle as the far end of the street grew clogged with bodies. The voices were a unified sound now, like a crowd at a stadium when the home team was at fourth and one. Peary couldn't hear anything but a sort of worshipful roar, but from this angle he could now see the news anchor on the television, a serious-faced man with a gloriously brown and glossy head of hair. The background picture showed a crowd much like the one down the street, but on the news, the focus was invisible. Angels didn't photograph, didn't show up on video. Rumors were that even artists who tried to sketch them ended up with random scribbles or blank canvases. Peary fancied the newsman looked a little lost and confused, talking inaudibly about angels. It would be nice if he really was confused, if Peary wasn't the only one who didn't understand. That was probably wishful thinking.

There was a sigh, a collective moan of disappointment, and a thousand pairs of eyes turned skyward, watching something invisible float away. After a moment of frozen silence, like flicking a switch, the visitation was over. Everyone dispersed almost as quickly as they'd gathered, in clumps and pairs now, whispering and hugging and clutching hands to hearts. Peary licked his lips, felt the sting, and watched them go. When the street was more or less back to normal (though the traffic wouldn't unsnarl for an hour or more, probably), Peary sidled over to the site of the angel's visit. He scoured the ground for the white handful he'd spotted, the locus of adoration, the angel.

There.

Peary picked it up: an old, off-white sweat sock with three blue stripes, slightly grubby from the gutter.

He glanced furtively around, tucked it in his coat pocket, and trotted away.

AT HOME, PEARY left the angel on the chair in the hall while he got his shoes off, hung his coat, washed his hands, and started a kettle for a cup of tea. Once he was warmed up and feeling more relaxed, he carried his mug with him to gather up the angel and take it to his trophy case in the spare room.

He called it the trophy case, anyway. It was mostly a joke. So far, the little shelf contained a pinecone, an old Slurpee cup (cherry, to judge by the residue), a baseball, and a fluorescent-pink home-made poster for some band he'd never heard of. In the corner of the room, beside Peary's laptop (his office, in the same way the shelf was his trophy case, and also mostly a joke these days), was a grocery store cart that had been an absolute beast to haul up the two flights of stairs to his apartment. Peary folded the sock neatly in half and tucked it between the pinecone and the cup.

Peary collected angels.

Every time he witnessed a visitation or heard of one close by, he waited it out patiently and gathered up the item that had sparked the sudden adulation, afterward dropped and forgotten like last year's hot Christmas toys. It was odd how those at the center of the crowd would lift up whatever it was that was being an angel at the time without seeming to notice that they were the ones doing the lifting. Peary wondered if it was similar at all to the way Ouija boards worked.

He flipped open his laptop and opened one of the dozens of .txt files that dotted the desktop. He typed a quick note—"Angel obj. = Ouija? subcons manip? Check journals re ideomotor effect"—and moved the window to one side. His screen was a mess; he had to clear some of this junk out. His computer always got more chaotic when he was out of work. For a while, he'd been able to keep focused by posting his thoughts and discoveries on atheist and freethinker websites, but as time had worn on, more and more people had just stopped posting there. Sometimes they left semi-coherent rants referencing everything from Buddha to prions to Saul's famous conversion on the road to Damascus, but in the end, they all saw the angels and left. Only Peary remained.

Peary typed another note. "Eschaton? Apocalypse?"

Maybe everyone else was right. Maybe the world would end now that the angels were arriving. Or returning.

He'd work on clearing out old files later.

Peary's television was usually set to one of the 24-hour news networks. Today, the screen filled with an image of a rapturous crowd singing a hymn. The voiceover identified it as a spontaneous gathering that had turned into a makeshift worship service, with random members of the crowd climbing up onto trees or benches or monuments and giving passionate sermons that they swore they hadn't planned. Some of them had spoken in tongues. Everyone had arrived in an orderly fashion, filing into the open and standing in neat ranks; a far cry from the scene Peary had witnessed. No one could explain it; they said they just felt moved to walk in a certain direction and the procession had crystallized around them. The panel of experts that came on after the raw footage thought that the visitations were getting more organized overall, as though whatever force was motivating them was getting better at it. Stronger. Knowing smiles were much in evidence. The lone dissenting voice, a tense woman with dark hair and sharp-edged glasses, gave a somewhat rambling explanation involving emergence, self-organization in complex chaotic systems, and a great deal of math. Peary didn't quite follow it, and it didn't look like anyone on the show was buying it, but he appreciated the effort. At least she was trying. He watched the rest of the segment, but they didn't use her name, and he turned the TV off when they cut to a piece on the economy.

Peary opened his laptop again and went looking for a browser game to play. Something simple and mindless. He didn't want to see anything else he didn't understand today.

The personalized and context-sensitive ads on his home page offered to connect him with his own guardian angel. He didn't click them.

PEARY HAD THREE cups of coffee and a foul-tasting energy shot for breakfast. he sat for a while in his "office," ostensibly working on an article – the same article he'd been working on for months, now long past deadline. He stared at his trophy case for a while. The objects arrayed along it were utterly ordinary. Peary couldn't even swear he'd know if someone swapped out, say, the pinecone when he wasn't looking. They were not pregnant with meaning. They did not whisper secrets. They just existed. He touched them, experimentally.

Solid.

He pulled on a sweater and went out.

Peary couldn't afford the bus anymore. His savings were drying up, and a freelancer's life was hardly Skittles and beer even at the best of times. He walked to the library instead, feeling the chill, smelling the exhaust and the distant echo of a departed hot dog vendor. The streets were quiet today, deserted. It felt like expectation. Peary didn't know what they were waiting for, couldn't know what everyone else knew, couldn't see the way they saw. His stomach rumbled and lurched, full of stimulants and acid, and he tried to ignore the lingering scent of pork by-product and sauerkraut.

The public library was quiet, too, but it was always quiet. No one read much anymore, especially not books. Revelation was faster than research and orders of magnitude more comforting. Just knowing things was what was cool now. Learning was for dinosaurs.

And also for Peary.

The bitterness, he knew, was in some ways the inevitable result of his shelf full of discarded angels and his sense of kinship with the tightly wound dark-haired woman on the news. He tried to accept the resentment and release it, to let himself feel and let the feelings pass. He had an intuition he wouldn't be able to, though.

The librarian nodded at Peary with a thin-lipped smile. She had a small television behind the counter and was glued to the latest news of angels; they had their own dedicated channel, now. At least her sense of duty had so far won out over her desire to wander the streets in search of enlightenment and spiritual healing. Peary nodded back and headed for the basement.

Paper, especially old paper, develops a characteristic smell as it ages, sometimes sour, sometimes bitter, always dusty. Peary could recognize some of his most-used books in the dark by now. He pulled his backpack open and tugged out his laptop. If he couldn't know it when he saw it, he could at least research it until he understood it. Chasing obscure references was rapidly becoming the only pleasure left within his diminished reach. He plugged in his computer. The screen flickered to life, a plain black background with notepad files like pigeon droppings, groups in clusters and spirals of his personal correlations. It was almost a diagram in itself. Peary had no idea what it meant.

He settled down to work.

THE FIRST HINT he had that something had gone wrong was when the lights went out. In the stacks, this meant Peary was plunged instantly into perfect darkness. His laptop beeped as it went to battery power, the dim blue-gray light of the screen now the only illumination available, making a puddle of light in the unbroken black. Peary sat in a tiny globe of solid space in a vast and intangible void. He hesitated. There was a muffled sound; more of a vibration, felt rather than heard. It reminded Peary of the naval base near his childhood home, when they fired the big guns during drills or demonstrations. He remembered feeling the ground tremble and wondering at it, tiny man-made earthquakes traveling from miles and miles away, their source hidden by the curvature of the planet.

Peary picked up his computer and disconnected the power cable. He left his papers and books where they lay. Using the screen as an awkward flashlight, he made his way carefully out of the basement and up to the first floor. The librarian was gone. The building was empty. From outside, he heard another rumble, sharper now, this one accompanied by a flash of light through the windows. Lightning? He set the laptop on a table and pushed out the front door.

Overhead, the clouds were black and furrowed, like plowed earth. Electricity crawled across them, branching lightning that never touched ground; dozens of hyperkinetic, glowing worms wriggled through the firmament. The streets were as empty as the library. No streetlights glowed. In the distance, Peary thought he could see movement. He glanced at the sky, then hunched his shoulders and went to find out. This was research, too; field research.

The crowds were packed like stacked marbles, like asparagus bundles, like pencils in a box. Peary hit the rear wall of people and could penetrate no further. He was too late, locked outside. Everyone was staring at something in the distance. No one spared him a glance, even when he tugged on their sleeves. Once, a pudgy matron with berries on her hat shushed him without turning her head. Lights flashed somewhere up there, and a finger of cloud was slowly wending down from overhead. A tornado? Here? Peary craned to see. Why weren't the crowds running? Where was the panic?

Lightning flashed again and again, a celestial strobe light. Peary felt as though the world was on pause, held in place while he scampered back and forth in the background. The crowd gasped suddenly, and Peary jumped like a child trying to see over his parents. The lightning stopped like a mouth snapping shut. Everyone fell to their knees, bowing, throwing themselves on their faces. Peary froze, unsure what to do. The crowd was still and silent, though still a crowd; someone coughed, and someone else shifted their knees arthritically on the asphalt.

Ahead, in the street, a figure appeared. Peary swallowed heavily. It was walking toward him. As it drew nearer in the half-light, he began to make out the details. A pale face with bright red lips. Red hair, short and curly. A yellow jumpsuit. Huge, floppy shoes.

"Ronald?" said Peary, unable to help himself.

"Lord, Lord!" came the murmur as the approaching apparition stepped daintily between the prostrate worshippers.

Peary's eyes darted from side to side as if trying to flee from his skull. Ronald was staring straight at him. Peary couldn't move, couldn't make his legs turn and carry him away. Wasn't sure if he even wanted to.

Ronald stepped free of the last of the crowd and stood before Peary. Peary met those terrible eyes, panic in his gut.

"It's a hap-hap-happy place," said Ronald. He spoke as if imparting some deep secret, some ultimate wisdom. He reached out and gripped Peary's shoulder. He smiled, but his eyes were sad, wide and brown and soulful as a cow's. "It's a clean and snappy place."

"Why?" Peary managed to gasp between dry lips.

"Have you had your break today?" Ronald extended his other hand. He held a hamburger, warm and fresh from the griddle. He pulled Peary's hands forward and deposited the burger in them. Hot grease dripped on Peary's wrists and burned there. Ronald held Peary's gaze for a moment longer, as though searching for something, some response, some glimmer of kindled understanding. He smelled of salt and greasepaint. "I'm lovin' it." His grip tightened. "I'm. Lovin'. It."

With a rustle of polyester, the clown turned and walked away. Peary held the burger and watched him go. Already, the crowds were turning, questions in their eyes. Peary saw hope, fear, anger, lust, the whole panoply of human emotion sprayed haphazardly across the sea of faces. The whispers started again, the questions, the desires, the need to know. Ronald had spoken to no one else. Only Peary held a gift from on high. He wasn't famous, not even Internet-famous. He was no one, a nonentity. He was everyone. He was a prophet.

Peary stood his ground as the crowd came back to themselves, as if awakening from a dream. His stomach gurgled; he never had gotten anything to eat that day.

Lifting the burger, Peary smelled the grade D meat and the soy filler, the rehydrated onions and the sour-sweet pickles, the tang of "fancy" ketchup and cheap yellow mustard. He wondered what it looked like to everyone else. He wondered if they saw the same thing he did.

He wondered if it mattered.

He took a bite.

It was delicious.

A Portrait of the Monster as an Artist

Dominik Parisien

For Helen Marshall

It knows poetry
is subjective, that one creature's poem
is the art that beats at the heart of another.

At times it fancies itself a fanged Eliot,
ripping subject from context
to gestate new meaning.

It remembers hungering
for a greater capacity for abstraction
gorging itself on organs of expression,
how as it ate it dreamt
of expanding to encompass thoughts
on all things that never were.

(It hears it mastered
only the delicate methods
of outrageous violence).

It believes an aesthetic
appreciation of the monstrous
is not for their like; that the day
they explore the canvas of its body
will reveal nothing
they would call wondrous.

It's a Universal Picture

Gwynne Garfinkle

1
I grew up loving witches:
peaked black hats and broomsticks for flight,
Bewitched and books about the Salem witch trials.
One Halloween I asked my dad to make me up.
He worked on me with pencil and putty,
then I looked in the mirror and burst into tears.
I'd wanted to be Elizabeth Montgomery.
He'd made me a warty hag.

2
Somehow my dad knew I would love
those black-and-white monster movies.
They didn't scare me:
Karloff and Lugosi, Colin Clive and Dwight Frye
(Clive died young of TB,
Frye of a heart attack, riding a bus),
Lon Chaney Jr. sorrowfully turning werewolf,
Gloria Holden as Dracula's Daughter
trying to fight her nature.
I watched them on TV Saturdays
before sessions in the dentist's chair,
my teeth pulled from overcrowded, crooked rows,
the taste of blood in my mouth.

3
When I was grown,
my bedridden dad, ravaged

and rewritten,
transformed by Parkinson's,
would snarl like Karloff's monster,
and I, in horror, turn away.

"Kid" Cooper
& the Blackwood Ape-Man

Adam Howe

We jumped off the train at dusk, hiking through the darkening woods till by full dark we reached a small settlement of tents inside a clearing. The forest was all sawed down to nubs around it, stacks of felled trees piled up like great wooden pyramids. It was quitting time at the logging camp. Pop collared a logger on his way to the saloon-tent, and asked the feller where we'd washed up, cuz it wasn't marked on Pop's map. "Blackwood," the man grunted, barging past us when he saw our bindles. "And Boss Taggart ain't hiring no hobos," he threw back over his shoulder.

Offended by the man's ill manners, Pop hurried us inside the saloon-tent. He eyed the room over. The usual strong backs sat hunched along the bar. Beery-red faces glared at us. Pop gave me the nod and I went into my sales pitch.

"I can't sing and I can't dance," I called out, "but I can whip any sonofabitch in town!"

I never liked speaking in public, and it'd taken some time, and many other working camps just like Blackwood, before I learned my lines without my voice shaking. Usually we could count on at least one drunk being so riled by my challenge that he bum-rushed me, and I'd lay out that jackass just to prove I meant business. After that, they'd bring up their best man. Bets would be called. A chalk-line scratched on the barroom floor. The crowd would form a living ring around us. And then we'd have at it till just one of us was left standing. After it was done, Pop'd count up our winnings, buy the losing man a drink to show there was no hard feelings, and then we'd be on our way, riding the rails to the next town.

But that's not what happened here.

No one took a swing at me. Instead the place went pin-drop quiet. The loggers drinking inside the tent only stared at us, all of them smiling the same queer smile, like they knew something me and Pop didn't.

"No man here will fight you," a voice growled from the shadows at the back of the tent. It belonged to a ruddy-faced hog of a feller; all that was missing was the apple in his mouth. He wasn't dressed like the other loggers, in their filthy working clothes; he wore a natty three-piece suit that strained against his bulging gut. He was sitting at a little round table with just a bottle of liquor for company. A cane was perched on his knee, to switch anyone who encroached on his privacy, or that bottle. He flicked a match with a thumbnail, firing up a cigar big as one of the trees laying out in the camp yard, the flame lighting his face like a jack-o'-lantern. He snuffed out the match with a dainty flick of his wrist. "But if it's a fight you're after." He blew a lasso of smoke above his head. "Then take it outside and I'll fetch you one."

The fat dandy's name was Boss Taggart. He led us outside the tent, strutting through the crowd like a prize rooster, carving a path through the jostling bodies with wicked switches of his cane, men yelping like scalded cats as it landed. Boss Taggart might not have been hiring—like the logger told Pop when we first come to Blackwood—but he surely believed in keeping his workers entertained; the men smelled blood, could hardly wait to see it spilled.

Marching through the crowd, I stripped off my shirt to the waist, Pop pushing and shoving to clear my way. Hollering over the noise—all that jeering and cussing—Pop gave me the usual game plan, and I nodded, said "Yup," made out I was listening. But it's hard to prepare without knowing first who you're fighting. If he's a slugger, a slickster, or a swarmer. And everyone's got a plan till they're punched on the nose. After that something else takes over: the animal that lives inside fighting men. A fighter's job is to keep that animal on its leash till it's time to let it loose n' wild.

Boss Taggart stopped suddenly, his cane tucked under his arm like a swagger stick. There was no boxing ring I could see, just a solid wall of men all around us. Violence baked off them like a brushfire burning out of control. I shot Pop a nervous look. The old man's expression did nothing to reassure me.

"What's the rumpus here, fellers?" Pop said.

Boss Taggart just stared at him, chewing his big ole cigar.

The crowd packed tighter around us.

"There's been talk of a ringer," Boss Taggart said, finally. "Young pup. About your boy's age." He stabbed the angry red eye of his cigar at me. "Riding the rails with an old man." Pop's chest puffed up at that 'old' business. "The way I hear it," Taggart said, "they been lickin' all comers and linin' their pockets, all the way up along the Trail."

"We wouldn't know nothing about that," Pop said. But he looked like a dog caught crapping on the porch.

BACK HOME, THEY'D called me "Kid" Cooper. Age sixteen, and I was about the most feared fighter in the county. I'd made my name in boxing booth bouts at the county fair, fighting grown men twice my size, dropping 'em cold with the corkscrew right hook that folks came to call my Widowmaker.

Kid kicks like a mule, Pop'd tell folks, a proud trainer.

Mama (when she found out I was fighting) hadn't approved, but she didn't say no to the prize money neither, cuz the bank was already circling our farm like a shark smelling blood, and the money I won helped hold them off for a spell, at least until Mama got sick and needed medicine.

By then the money wasn't enough, for Mama or the bank.

No one hits as hard as life, Pop used to say. And life never hit harder than the fall of '33, the week we lost Mama to the fever, and then the bank took our farm. Talk about your one-two punch. Life sure can stick it to you sometimes. I tried to stay strong like Pop told me. Bit down on my gum shield and soaked up the pain. Cuz it wasn't just us. Folks was hurting all over in them days. We'd see 'em sometimes, starved scarecrows dressed in rags, dirt caked in the cracks of their old-too-soon faces, skulking along to Lord knows where. Someplace better they hoped. But where was that anymore?

We buried Mama under the old sycamore, on land we no longer owned, and then Pop packed our bindles, with my boxing mitts in mine, and we hit the road.

Since then we'd been hoboing north through the mountains, riding the rails or our thumbs when we could, tramping when we couldn't, passing through working towns and putting my God-given talent to use in the prize ring.

Pop told me, I kept winning the way I was, by the time we reached the city I'd have served my apprenticeship and be ready for the pros.

One day, he said, *you'll be Heavyweight Champ of the world.*

But before that was Blackwood, where it seemed my reputation had preceded me.

Boss Taggart offered his terms, smiling a smile that never reached his eyes.

It was the biggest wager I'd ever heard. Crazy money. All we had. Everything I'd won. But before I could stop it, talk some sense into Pop, he'd shook Taggart's hand to seal the deal. Maybe it was the talk of ringers that shamed Pop into taking such a damn-fool bet, cuz it's a fine line between a ringer and a grifter, and Pop prided himself on being a good honest Christian. Or maybe Pop was afraid what the crowd would do if he *didn't* take the bet. Whatever it was, it was too late now.

Pop wiped his hand that'd shook with Boss Taggart on the leg of his pants, like he'd just made a deal with Old Scratch. "Alright," he said, "now who are we fighting? Where's your man? Bring him up!"

With a twirl of his cane, Boss Taggart pointed past the crowd, the loggers shuffling aside like he was Moses parting the Red Sea. As the last of the men moved away, I saw a giant wooden door embedded in the ground. Solid oak. Bolted shut with a rusted steel bar. Like some kind of storm shelter, or the world's biggest root cellar. Boss Taggart strode through the crowd and out onto the door, the heels of his boots clacking on the oak, the wood groaning under his bulk.

"Must've been a couple-few years back," he said, slashing his cane in the air like a carny barker. "When we first started grubbing these woods, the camp cook come told me, someone was breaking into the storehouse at night and helping hisself to our food rations. Now, my boys know better than to steal from me." Taggart glared around at his workers, who nodded and murmured their agreement. "So I figured it's gotta be some runaway chain-gang nigger. Cuz whoever it was left his bare footprints in the dirt outside the storehouse. And they was *big*." He gave a chuckle and the crowd brayed like jackasses, like it was some kind of joke me and Pop weren't privy to. "Now if there's one thing I can't stand, it's a thief," Boss Taggart proclaimed, "and if there's another, it's a nigger. So I set a trap for that stealin' black sumbitch. And I caught him, alright. 'Cept it wasn't no nigger like I thought."

With that, Taggart stamped his boot on the oak door.

The hellish cry that came back—like some roaring beast from the Book of Revelations—turned my blood to ice.

Stepping off the door, Taggart gave his men the nod.

The huge steel bolt was slammed back, the door hauled up on thick rope. A black cloud of flies billowed out behind it. A fetid animal stink wafted up from the pit. I staggered back, retching, my eyes watering at the stench. I swiped the flies from my face, not believing what I was seeing down below.

Huddled in the gloomy pit was some kind of ape. I'd seen one before at the carny, something like this, only much smaller. It was hard to believe they was even related. This 'un had to be seven foot tall, easy. It was tethered to an iron post in the middle of the pit. A rusted length of chain dangled between the post and the leather choker the ape wore 'round its neck. Its coarse black hair was mangy in patches, and crawling with so many lice it looked like the wind was blowing its fur. Its body was a mess of scars, some old and faded white, others fresher and festering, all courtesy of a whip or—I thought more likely—Boss Taggart's cane.

The ape peered up from the shadows of the pit, glaring hatefully at the jeering crowd, its mud-brown eyes pitted in a shovel-flat, leathery black face. Its head was a boulder on broad slab-like shoulders, its arms like something the loggers had felled, stretching damn near the length of the pit. Its ham-hock fists were clad in boxing gloves, the thick black leather all chewed up, as if the ape had taken to gnawing at the gloves like a dog with an old slipper. He was wearing a pair of ragged old long-shorts, crudely stitched from oilskin, probably from a tent; and I could tell he was a he on account of the bulge at the front—else he had a snake stuffed down there he was keeping warm.

The ape saw me up in the crowd and growled, baring teeth that were filed down to nubs, just like the trees around camp. Thick ropes of saliva drizzled off his chops in a mad dog foam. I teetered back in shock, bumping into Pop, who clutched at my arm in terror.

"Don't you worry 'bout those teeth none," Boss Taggart told me. "He don't bite." He seemed to consider this. "Well, he might nibble you a bit, I s'pose," he allowed. "We caught this ole boy at a good young age—I figure he wasn't much more than a pup when we snared him—and we taught him right." He whapped his cane in his hand and the ape flinched at the sound. "So it mightn't be Queensbury rules exactly," Taggart said, "but you'll get a fairish fight."

"Taggart," Pop said, "you must be crazy, you think I'd send my boy down there with that damned thing!"

He took a step towards Taggart, holding out his hand.

"Bet's off," Pop said. "Now you give us back our money—"

Taggart's cane slashed down on Pop's palm. Pop let out a yelp, snatching his hand to his chest, shocked as a scolded child. In the next swipe, the cane scythed across Pop's jaw, knocking him to the ground. I crouched down beside him. He was bleeding at the mouth, dazed, his eyes rolling in different directions. A cold fury burned through me. I glared up at Taggart, ready to pounce—

He was grinning, holding a pistol on me.

"Save your energy, scrapper."

"I won't fight," I told him.

Taggart's shark's smile widened. "Either you fight him, like was shook on—or we toss your pappy down in there instead."

Pop squeezed my hand weakly. "Don't listen to him, son, you don't gotta do nothing," he rasped. But he didn't sound none too confident. I brushed his hair back off his face, bent down and kissed his forehead. Then I stood up.

I looked Taggart hard in the eye. "Are you a man of your word, mister?"

The question seemed to confuse him.

"I want your word," I said, "that when I whip this monster of yours, you'll hand over our winnings and let us leave here."

Well, that tickled him plenty; he threw back his head and roared with laughter.

But he finally quit laughing, and shook my hand.

"Sure, kid. Whatever you say."

I wiped my hand on the leg of my pants, just like Pop'd done: shaking hands with Boss Taggart was like petting a toad. Then I looked around at the loggers. "You all heard him," I called out loud, so even the men at the back of the crowd could hear; and my voice was *not* shaking. "He gave his word."

I laced up my mitts.

"First you gotta win, boy," Boss Taggart sneered. "And my '*monster*' ain't never been beat."

A ladder was lowered into the pit. The hole was twelve foot by twelve, and eight foot deep; like something the devil hisself had clawed up from the ground. At each corner of the pit, torches burned up on flagpoles, the flames lighting the hole like a vision of hell. I started down the ladder, glancing back to see Pop being hauled to his feet. Boss Taggart slung an arm around Pop's shoulder like they was bosom buddies. Pop's head was clearing. He gave me a little nod for luck—or maybe it was goodbye?

Descending into the pit, I could hear the loggers making their side-bets. No one was giving me hardly any chance at all. The ladder was yanked up behind me. Down in the pit, the smell was worse than ever. The ground was strewn with a rancid mess of rotten vegetables and ape-shit.

The ape stood up, and up, and up; towering over me. His little jug ears flicked at some flies buzzing 'round his head. The beast's back was hunched from so much time spent huddled in the pit, his shoulders ridged with thick quivering muscle. His body looked carved from teak, those tree-trunk arms dangling down past his knees. Glaring at me, the ape gave an angry snort of breath that frosted in the cold night air. He started pacing 'round the pit on his chain, stomping his canoe-size feet in the dirt.

Between the hollering crowd and my own hammering heart, I could hardly think straight, get it clear in my mind what I needed to do. I told myself that a creature his size couldn't be fast. I'd stick and move, let him chase me; tire him out before pulling the trigger and putting him to sleep—if I could.

But the moment Boss Taggart called "Fight!" robbed me of that notion.

Damn, he was quick.

He lashed out a jab that snapped my head back, spreading my nose across my face like butter on bread. My legs did a dance like a jazz club Negro. I'd never felt nothing like it. It shook me right down to the soles of my boots. And this was just a jab! I shook my head to clear my vision—

Just in time to see the uppercut surging towards me like some leviathan from the deep. It detonated on my chin, hurling me back off my feet. I thudded against the hard dirt wall of the pit, sliding down it, landing heavy on my ass.

The crowd cheered.

The ape charged.

Head still swimming, I could only watch, helpless, as it thundered across the pit towards me, before the chain tethering it to the post snapped tight, stopping the beast in its tracks. A fist like a leather-wrapped wrecking ball whistled past my face, ruffling my hair. The ape waddled back like a drunken sailor, releasing the pressure of the choker around its neck, the tether-chain going slack.

Bracing myself against the wall, I spat blood, and then heaved myself up onto rubbery legs. Knowing he couldn't reach me with my back to the wall, I circled around the giant, looking for an opening. There was plenty of him to hit; it was what he threw back that worried me—I'd barely recovered from that jab, let alone the upper-cut. I kept circling, getting dizzy. The crowd cussed and heckled my tactics—I heard Boss Taggart say to Pop he had a sissy for a son—but to hell with them, I was just trying to survive down there.

The ape circled 'round with me, windmilling those tree-trunk arms, nearly blowing me off my feet as they devilled past. I started to wonder if the sonofabitch would ever tire, cuz I was sure feeling the pace. I needed to do something—*fast*—before I gassed or my fear overwhelmed me.

Still circling, I started timing his shots, the old training coming back. I bobbed and weaved—that seemed to confuse him—then I darted inside and hit him a solid shot to the breadbasket, darting back out to the wall before he could counter. I kept it going. Circling. Darting in. Hitting him hard and fast with everything I had. Darting back out before he could tag me.

But my best shots didn't even faze him; all they did was piss him off and hurt my hands. And every so often he'd catch me a good 'un before I could get out of range, and I'd *know* I'd been caught. My knees would buckle and the world would cartwheel, a black veil fluttering before my eyes. Behind that black veil I'd see Mama standing out under the sycamore where we'd left her, the setting sun bleeding across the horizon behind her. She was smiling sadly, like she hadn't expected to see me again so soon.

I don't know how long we had at it. No rounds were ever called. It felt like forever. My face must've looked like I'd gone bobbing for apples in a hornet's nest. My mouth felt like I'd been chewing broken glass. Half of my teeth were studding the ape's gloves. My lungs burned, my broken nose whistling as I snorted for air. Blood streamed in my eyes where the brows had split like peapods, blinding me, but I just swiped my face with my gloves and fought on.

Then he pole-axed me with a jab that felled me to my knees.

Pop used to tell me, *A champion is someone who gets up when he can't.* But I was done. I couldn't beat this thing. On my hands and knees, crawling in bloody mud and ape-shit, I gazed up from the pit, filled with a shame I'd never known. My blurring eyes found Pop amid the frenzied crowd. Boss Taggart was gloating. He still had his arm around Pop, the pistol cradled in his hand, patting Pop's chest like a deadly promise. The fear in Pop's eyes cleared my head like a dose of smelling salts.

I sucked a deep ragged breath, and hauled myself to my feet.

The ape backed up a step, maybe surprised at my sand. Then he pounded his gloves together, the leather clapping like thunder, and came back at me.

Launching myself off the wall, I met him head-on. Ducking under his arms and bulling my way to his body. Chopping him with hooks that cratered his midsection. Pounding his ribs till they cracked. Grinding my knuckles in the splintered bone. Roaring with pain, the ape threw me off him. I bounced off the wall and sprang to my feet. I'd hurt him, at last, and if he could be hurt, he could be beat. I swarmed back in and kept mauling his body. Up close, his arms were too long to do me much damage; best he could do was clinch and avalanche his weight down on me, though that was plenty, my tired legs buckling under the strain.

He wrestled me into a clinch, clamping my face in his swampy armpit, bristles raking my eyes like he was lacing me with his gloves. Well, if he was gonna fight dirty, then so was I. I stomped my heel down hard on his foot and he let out a howl and released me. As he staggered back, I sledged a shot to his liver that woofed the wind out of him, and he grabbed hold of his tether-post for balance.

I swooped back in. He was covering up now, trying to protect his cracked ribs from my hooks, leaving his head unguarded—just like I wanted.

Feinting with a left to the body, he dropped his guard and I suckered him with my Widowmaker. Right on the button. Point of the chin. Lord knows where I found that punch; and if God don't know then the devil surely does, cuz it flew straight from hell. The ape's head snapped back, spraying sweat and lice. It damn nearly sprang off his shoulders, out of the pit and up into the crowd. The ape's arms flailed. His eyes rolled over white in his skull. And then he hit the deck with a crash, the ground quaking beneath him, loose dirt raining down from the walls of the pit.

Standing over the fallen giant, I got an idea how David must've felt when he whipped Goliath. I went to raise my arms but didn't have no energy left. I sank to my knees in exhaustion. Looking down at the ape, his great hairy chest heaving as he snorted for breath, and then up at the crowd, bug-eyed and hollering for blood, I couldn't decide which was more beast-like.

In the confusion, Pop fought free of Boss Taggart and dropped the ladder into the pit. He scrambled down it, dragging me into his arms and then hoisting me onto his shoulders, carrying-on like he'd never had no doubt I'd pull through. Boss Taggart spat out his cigar—it probably didn't taste so fine now—and came down the ladder behind him, the pistol hanging loose by his side. He couldn't bring himself to look at me as he passed; just tossed a heavy coin-purse, with our wager and the winnings, at my feet. Pop snatched up the purse and pocketed it. Taggart waded through the bloody mud, crossing the pit and standing over the ape, cursing it. Then he raised his pistol and thumbed back the hammer.

It sickened me that Taggart would just kill it in cold blood, this beast who'd fought braver than any man I'd ever known.

That's something about fighters; you can go life and death with a feller, but after it's over, he's your brother in blood.

"Wait!"

Taggart looked over at me.

"You let that critter go now," I said.

He gave a little snort. "The hell you say."

He started raising the pistol again, but I caught his arm at the wrist, and he bit back a yelp as I squeezed. We fought for the pistol, the gun barrel hovering over the fallen ape, Taggart's finger teasing the trigger. After battling the ape, I was damn near spent, and Taggart knew it. His jack-o'-lantern face lit up as he started getting the upper hand. Then I wrenched his arm and his shoulder popped so loud for a moment I thought he'd fired off a shot. Taggart shrieked in pain. I tore the pistol from him, and he staggered back, shroud-white and sweating, his dislocated arm dangling from the socket by a thread. He tripped over his feet and fell on his ass in a big pile of ape-shit. Someone in the crowd above us gave a wild hoot of laughter; I wondered if the feller would still have a job tomorrow.

"I'll see you hang for this, you sonofabitch—" Taggart hissed. "You, your old man, *and* that damned abomination!"

I pointed the pistol at him.

Taggart shut up right quick and closed his eyes, whimpering.

I held that pistol on him for some time, not sure what I was going to do.

And then I turned and shot through the chain tethering the ape to the post. Sparks spit and the broken chain dropped from the post, coiled in the mud like a rusty snake. Boss Taggart started sobbing. He looked scared enough to be adding to that big pile of shit he was sitting in. I stuffed the pistol in my waistband.

I kneeled down next to the ape, petting his big bristly head to let him know I meant him no more harm. He looked at me and gave a little grunt like he understood. When I tore off his ragged old gloves, he gave an all too human sigh of relief, rubbing his huge leathery hands together like he was trying to warm them. Then I removed the leather choker from his throat. Under the choker, the fur was worn away, the skin gray and raw like a mangy cur. I flared with anger at how Taggart how mistreated this wretched creature, and for forcing me to add to his misery.

With the last of my strength, I helped the ape back to his feet. Still groggy, he steadied himself against the iron post, and rubbed his throat where the choker had been. Something like understanding flashed across his face. He seemed to realise he was free. He looked up out of the pit and roared at the men peering down at him. In the blink of an eye, there wasn't a logger to be seen, just the dust of their fleeing feet. The ape turned back towards Boss Taggart—cowering in terror and shit—and started stomping around him, growling down low in his throat and bunching his wrecking ball fists. It seemed he had one last fight left in him. One last score to settle.

But me and Pop had seen enough.

We climbed the ladder up out of the pit, and started out of Blackwood, Pop with his arm around me, helping me along. No one tried to stop us. Frightened eyes peered out from tents as we passed. Boss Taggart's high, hog-like squeals echoed over the camp behind us. Pop didn't look back, didn't even slow down. But I did. The last thing I saw before my swelling eyes puffed shut, was the ape vaulting up from the pit and loping away through the camp till he vanished in the woods. He was carrying something. Something round and dripping red, his fingers sunk into it like a bowling ball. My swollen eyes pinched shut before I could tell what it was. And maybe that's for the best.

Pop guided me back through the woods to the rail-line where we'd first hopped off the train. Dawn birds were chirping. On the next train to pass, we hitched a ride and travelled the rest of the way to the city without any more stops, not saying a word about what'd happened in Blackwood.

Patching me up in the boxcar, Pop told me he was proud of me. I was ready for the pros, he said. That was good to hear; I hated to think what else I'd have to do to prove my mettle. We made it to the city and I won my first pro bout KO1 and we never looked back. And the rest, my journey to the title and my reign as Heavyweight Champ—well, the rest is in the sports record books.

After fighting the ape-man of Blackwood, it was a cinch.

Bearing Witness

Jane Yolen

We have all had the teeth at our throats.
Even you, princess, gnawed by time,
and the memory of the weight of crowns.
Even you, hero of the moment, your sword
and sword-hand still red with a stranger's blood.
Even you, storyteller, myth-maker, wind-writer,
the stained fonts of your reviews before you,
your best work like a long tail behind.
The teeth marks may be invisible, but still they ache.
We all need to own the story of our lives,
bear witness, weep down the moon, iterate,
move on.

Otter Script

Alex Dally MacFarlane

what script scratched on stone
above bones like a weave:
humerus-warp and spine-weft
and nested there the otters' ghosts
among spraint and bones
scratching stones like ancient hands:
what script? what meaning-lost lines?
old words or old patterns,
ghosts of old clothes, disintegrated
in the bones of a 5000-year-old tomb:
what stories sunk in mud?

A Primer for Reading 23 Pairs of Chromosomes, or, Introduction to Your Own Personal Genome Project

Jeannine Hall Gailey

You are not a ticking time bomb.
Your results feel more like collage art,
a Frankenstein patchwork mostly unproblematic.
Yes, a carrier gene for this, a likelihood for that—an old age
of macular degeneration, a possible thyroid cancer—
but this book's chapters carry you in fascinating directions—
thousands of years into the past, exotic destinations and origins:
Ireland, Norway, France, even the Middle East and Africa.
Your skin color a trick of the light. Your statistics
are not so glum, and is it a delight or disappointment
to find you might have been born a blue-eyed blonde
instead of a grey-eyed brunette? To find a high pain tolerance
and no tendency towards alcoholism? Oh, speak to us,
amino-acid chains, and tell us our futures. Pretend for a moment
not to know our dark secrets, our fading memories
for foremothers. Embrace the order of things: traits
that take three neat pairings, a bleeding tendency ticked
on or off. A heart flutter your grandmother also experienced,
your great-aunt's straight nose and high forehead.
Sail into the future armed with the knowledge you refused
ignorance of your own body's demons and delights,
that your home country is fairy tale, ice and reindeer and green sheets
of rain, the sand of Brittany, the mountains of Tennessee.

Dualities

Rose Lemberg

The universal flow of prime numbers
unleashed from your/my sleeves
surrounds you/me in pillars of light. I/you never
understood math, you/I never
knew much about architecture, languages,
the processing of speech into data and storysong, that
wordshaping that anchored me/you in the ground. You/I navigate
between stars with motion/no motion
that exists outside timeflow and yet bound in it; the manifold,
    unfolding
along the pathways of the veins.

You/I understand little
of the laws that frame me/you, and yet
we broke up with the fathers of our children, wept/silently grit teeth
over our sons' disabilities, kept quiet/spoke
over the screams of the body, took
new lovers
in an attempt/absolution over despair/despair.

you/I, emergent and merged
through this language, this silence, this memory of forgetting,
through kinetic numbers and the accumulation of sung lives:
I/you, traversing this desert/this space
shall speak/sing with hope ascendant.

Falling upward, you/I will not merge
into a cohesion not of our designing. We will exist/be

wound against each other in pillars of light,
like DNA or prime numbers,
like rivers,
like storysongs into the earth,
at the exit/entrance to the worlds that are becoming.

Salamander

Alicia Cole

a black snake, he said, crouching
in the dark; then, its tiny feet shuffled
like smudges of oil

crouching, our bodies echoed the night
smoked in grey, his mouth quite clear

my husband joined us, fingers loose
at his hip; the salamander quickened
its pace into the grass

loose, my husband's fingers clicking
pictures, flick of a sinuous tail

moistened, a baffled Pliny states,
the salamander appears inside fire,
its body draining the heat

states: three mouths moistened, startle,
the salamander dancing, dark and sooty

lit like candles in the night, the light of
our bodies tied, triumvirate; small creatures,
struggling

Pureland

Livia Llewellyn

The Closed Unsink

Half an hour after Darin, Laith and Mal went downstairs for more beer, Exene knew something was wrong. It was a five minute walk to the nearest on-campus store—where the hell were they? Exene stumbled to her feet and wandered the gloomy halls of the unfamiliar dorm, her drunken fuzz disappearing as the silence grew. The air smelled of cigarettes and paint molding off damp walls, but that wasn't anything new. Still, something had happened, intuition told her. Traces of a cut-off sound lingered in the air, the kind of silence following thunderstorms, when the alien city lay shocked into submissive, uneasy peace. Something had happened.

She found them in the basement laundry room, standing over the body of the girl. Except, it wasn't a girl, Darin insisted. "That's not Kylie. It's just her shell."

Exene stared at the girl. She was a sophomore, from one of the floors in her own cinderblock dorm, far across campus. Just another offworlder like Exene, a girl who liked to drink and fuck. Tonight she was a girl with a slightly deflated body. Rivers of flat beer and broken glass lay around her, an emerald and amber cape. Her skirt had been flung up, revealing smooth skin, sticky-wet. Exene stepped back, her nails biting into her fists.

"You raped her?"

"No!" Laith's voice cracked. "I swear, we didn't do anything—"

"She came onto us," Darin said. "She wanted us to buy her booze, in exchange for blow jobs. She suggested down here—"

"—so no one would see," finished Mal. "We didn't force her to do anything. She totally wanted it."

Exene stared at the body, then looked up at the boys. Laith's jeans were unzipped, and his belt buckle clinked against the metal teeth.

"She was going to blow all of you? Just for booze?"

"I swear, we didn't hurt her—not at first, not until—"

"She doesn't believe us," Mal said, silencing Laith. The boys looked at each other. "Show her."

No one moved.

"Show me."

Darin reached down with a shaking hand, and pulled Kylie's left foot out of her shoe. The leg flattened like rubber, long and smooth. Exene's mouth opened, but only a low moan escaped. Darin curled the toes, followed by the foot itself all the way to the heel, then started on the calf, pressing the air up through the rubbery body as he rolled her leg like a carpet. The air escaped Kylie's mouth in a low sigh, as if tired of the demonstration.

"She's a fruit roll-up." The words tumbled out of Darin's mouth. Mal giggled, a high-pitched sound that died against the concrete walls.

"No bones. No anything inside." Darin stopped at her knee, then let go and stood up. The flesh held in a soft spiral for several seconds, then unfurled in a languid wave. "See?"

"Yeah. I get it now." Exene turned away to one of the large metal sinks, and threw up. It didn't help. Her vomit only reminded her of the mess behind her—specks of flesh spattered across white washers, droplets of blood shining on the boy's faces and clothes. The air smelled like rancid fat and dryer sheets. Exene gagged, but clamped her lips tight. She had to keep it together, even though she was freaking out, and didn't really get any of this at all.

"You study dead people, right? This is right up your alley, you can help us. Are you gonna help us?"

Exene turned the faucet on and cupped her hands, first washing out her mouth, then cleaning the sink with splashes of iron-flecked water. Dark chunks swirled around and down, disappearing into the wide holes of the drain. Some of them caught, and Exene used her fingers to push the soft sick through. It didn't bother her. It was just from her body, after all, and she was used to cleaning up messes like that. That's what you did when you were human. You got used to it. It's what you were.

She knew what she had to do.

"I need a plastic bag, something small that we can roll her up into, and duct tape. Also, lots of rags and cleaner. Bleach, if you have it. Geez, you guys made such a mess. Couldn't you have just shot her?" It was a disgusting joke, but Exene let herself pass from horror into delirium. It was the only way she could cope.

Mal shrugged. "We were drunk."

"That's no excuse. When aren't you drunk?"

"She wouldn't stop moving." Laith gulped back a sob. He looked like he was going to pass out. "Her arms kept growing and growing, she was all over me. I couldn't unwrap her—" His hands scraped up and down his arms, as if trying to exorcise some invisible trace of the girl still clinging to his skin. "It was like getting caught in seaweed. She wouldn't let go. Her mouth kept opening wider, and she just wouldn't let go—"

"Besides, we didn't have a gun," Darin chimed in. He was the cutest of the three, but only by a margin. Exene had a hard time telling them apart, even though she spent almost every day in the library with them. She knew she'd wanted to fuck one of them tonight, which was why she'd agreed to come over and have a few beers. But wait—wasn't it Laith she'd wanted to screw? It didn't matter now. She never wanted to see them again.

"We don't have all night. Get the stuff. Laith, stay outside the door. Don't let anyone else in."

The boys filed out in silence, only Laith looking back with horror as he closed the door. Exene sat on one of the dryers and stared at the mess below her feet. All her fear had fled with the last of her puke, and now curiosity burned through her, bright and clean. Kylie lay on the floor like an abandoned pupa, an unfinished sentence. Somewhere in the boy's wet mouths, in the warren of unlit rooms, an unspoken ending lay hidden. Under the harsh florescent lights, Exene stared at the paper-thin girl cloaked in the amber-emerald cape, willing her to somehow rise up and whisper the answer, the end to the sentence. But there was nothing left of her, at least not enough to speak. Only folded skin, shadows and creases—directions of a sort, if you knew how to read them, if you could unfold or fold them the right way.

"You're the answer," Exene whispered. "I just have to learn how to read you."

Ten minutes later, the door handle clicked, and the boys crept in one by one. Darin clutched a waterproof sleeping bag cover in one hand.

"It's small, but if we roll her up—" he said.

"Give it to me. I'll do it." Darin and Mal didn't argue as Exene slid off the dryer and grabbed the bag from his hand, then kneeled onto the floor.

"She's really dead, isn't she?" Laith asked.

"Yeah." Hesitant, her hands hovered over the flesh. What would it feel like?

"We can help," Mal began, but Exene knew he was lying.

"It's ok," she said as she began to caress the skin into a soft coil. "I'll get rid of her body. You do the rest." The boys sighed in relief as they backed away, already ignoring her, already joking, laughing. Beneath Exene's moving hands, Kylie sighed once more. Boys are all the same, she seemed to say.

The Twist Fold

Exene didn't get rid of the girl. She took Kylie back to her dorm, tucked neatly in her backpack next to the last six-pack of beer, weeping condensation from the warmth. The boys would never need to know.

The Open Double Sink

"I heard she dropped out of school."

The toothbrush in Exene's mouth slowed as she picked up snatches of conversation on the other side of the bank of sinks. Green foam bubbled at her lips, threatening to spill onto her chin, but she ignored it.

"That wouldn't surprise me. It's not like she ever went to classes. I don't know why she even bothered to be here."

"She likes college cock."

"Don't we all."

Witchy laughter bounced off the chipped tiled walls. Exene leaned over the sink and spat.

"Has anyone been in her room? She has, like, five of my shirts."

"Just wait another week. Her parents pay for everything, she'll show up when she runs out of money and has to beg for more. There's nowhere else for her to go."

Exene turned the water on and bent over the sink. Out of the corner of her eye she watched two girls round the bank, pausing to stare at her before they disappeared into the hall. "Prairie whore," one whispered, the words lingering like steam.

Ignoring them, Exene tapped her brush and turned off the water, grabbed her tube of paste, and pushed open the door. It was well after midnight, and the labyrinthine hallway lay empty, filled only with faint echoes of the girls' voices. She hurried back to her room, barely opening it enough to squeeze in before locking it tight behind her. Better safe than sorry.

In the dark, Exene felt her way over to the window, raised the blinds, and cracked open a grimy pane. Beyond the feral borders of the wooded campus, an ocean-bound megalopolis spread out in all directions to a dun horizon spiked by neon-tipped steel. Slow-moving lights streamed in lines of red and gold, like wires being pulled from a carpet of deep grey. Constant murmuring of machinery and engines, sirens and horns—Exene pressed her cheek against the cold glass, comforted by the sounds. When she'd entered the floating city six years ago, after spending two centuries cocooned in a decrepit SLT cruiser, she thought she'd be overwhelmed by the sheer size of the place, the never-ending panoply. Sometimes, when she ventured away from the urban oasis of the campus, she still was. But in these quiet moments in the middle of the night, it soothed her, like the distant rainstorms of her quiet, empty homeworld. Those girls were right: at her core, she was still prairie.

A bitter-cold gust pushed past her, and papery whispers rose from the corner of the room. Exene closed her eyes. She knew what that sound was from. Behind her, Kylie swayed. Exene had clipped the body to a skirt hanger, and every evening for a month, she'd taken her from a garment bag in her closet and hung her on the hook behind the door, letting the flesh dry in the winter air. Kylie's skin had cured to thick paper, dry but flexible, creamy and dappled like an elegant invitation. Exene turned, stared at the O's of Kylie's eyes, the gaping lip-lined mouth. Every night at this time, with the wind blowing through the room, Exene fearfully hoped Kylie would break her silence, tell her what happened. Not tonight, it seemed.

Exene drew the blinds, then turned on the lamp as she settled down before her homework. Two sagging shelves of textbooks cast shadows onto a desktop cluttered with papers and journals, essay exams marked heavily in red ink, notes from classes and symposiums. She needed to study, had to study, her student loans depended on it. The people and planet she left behind depended on it. Kylie's hollow stare pressed hard against Exene's neck, sliding beneath her flesh down to the bone. Exene shivered, eased a fat anatomy book from the shelf, and flipped through it. This was homework, of a sorts.

Ink outlines of bones and muscles, detailed and delicate, flowed past her fingers as she turned each page. Eldritch, human and xeno anatomies, as open as lovers, displayed veins and vessels and mounds of organs with dispassionate, painless precision. What kind of clues she sought in those cartographies of flesh, she couldn't say. The drawings were complex, ornate, weighty. Exene rubbed her stomach, aware of coiled masses and sticky fluids bound beneath the thin layer of skin. What had happened to Kylie was the exact opposite. She'd opened up, and everything flew away, leaving her purged, uncomplicated, pure.

The black phone on her bedstand shuddered out a death rattle ring. Exene grimaced, but she knew it wouldn't stop until she answered. She reached behind her and scooped the heavy receiver off the stand. "What."

"We need to talk."

One of the boys, she didn't know which one. They'd all sounded the same. After they helped her clean up the laundry room, they'd seemed anxious to never speak about it again. She should have known better. They must have followed her home that night. Something bad was going to come of this—she felt it deep in the thumping muscle that supposedly housed her soul. That's why she gave them the same answer every night he called.

"I told you a thousand times, I didn't tell any one, so fuck off. It's over, leave me alone."

. . . leave me alone.

"But you already lied about getting rid of her. What else did you lie about? We can't trust you. Give her back."

"I don't have time for this shit."

. . . time for this shit.

The bad connection echoed her words in static whispers, as if acting out the conversation for unseen listeners hovering on the lines.

"We're going to get her, whether you like it or not. Stupid bitch." In the background, boozy laughter. "Cunt."

Exene rolled her eyes and hung up. Once they started with the profanities, the conversation, such as it was, always devolved. Still, she had to smile. He'd said the word as if he'd just discovered it, with all the fresh acidic joy of a child popping a stick into the eyes of an animal carcass. She turned back to her books, but the mood was broken. After a few minutes, she closed the onionskin pages. Up on the shelf, in front of two hard-won undergrad diplomas, a framed photo of her parents stared down at their only daughter, their weathered faces as hard as the land behind them—Exene was never unaware of their presence, blessing and cursing her. It had been her dream to be a doctor, someone who could save her people from the alien rot that nibbled at their bones. Except, there were no universities on their planet, only continents of grasses and grains, and the vast machines that harvested them. So her parents traded a round-trip ticket and two decades of schooling for her solemn promise to return and help solve the medical mysteries of a desolate farming planet becoming more casket than breadbasket. They were long dead now, transmuted by alien cancers into the very land they'd tilled, fertilizer for mimetic weeds and carnelian-colored corn.

They'd changed, just like Kylie. And Exene was changing too. The solid sleep of space had arrested her life—but only momentarily, and this wild new world and sprawling city were reforging her. The promise she made centuries ago was working itself from under her skin, just like Kylie's bones. A single thought, once a droplet in an ocean of expectations, had become a constant trickle in the back of her mind. Exene turned off the light and opened the blinds again. Soon the trickle would look like the city's horizon—wide and rushing, uncontainable. Beauty and blight inerasable, changing the landscape of her life forever.

"It's been too long," Exene said to her glass reflection. "I don't think I can keep my promise."

. . . *keep my promise.*

Exene turned, ice-water slow. Kylie glowed, her hollow skin holding the city light like a waxy candle shell. Exene walked over, rose on her toes and whispered into the pale mouth.

"Forgive me. I'm changing."

Kylie rustled, catching the sounds and playing them back like dune grass mimicking the kiss of the wind.

. . . *i'm changing.*

The Water Bomb Base

Cross-legged, Exene sat on the remains of a rusted bench at a desolate, undeveloped edge of the waterfront of Serpentine Bay, one of seventeen long and curving bays that gave the city its starfish shape. Below the legs of the bench, the ground sloped away and disappeared under a massive jumble of weather-worn stone blocks, ancient and eons-old ruins of the city's original buildings and foundations, carved by a long-extinct race. At this bleak stretch of the waterfront, it was rumored that if the waves drew back far enough, you could make out the face of a colossal statue, wave-smooth and hollow-eyed. Whether the face was human or something else, no one had ever said.

Boo, her boyfriend of last summer—her ex now—perched on the bench's edge beside her, smoothing his herringbone wool skirt over cabled leggings. She handed him half her sandwich, and they ate in silence while looking across the bay, at a skyline glistening under light afternoon rains. They'd met last summer, bumping into each other during a hot night of searching for parties on the nearly empty campus, and had been inseparable until fall semester—even now, he was still her closest friend, the only person she could confide in. The fact that they broke up the day after Boo revealed he was transitioning to female was merely a coincidence. Studying was her life, Exene told him, she had no time for anything else. Boo didn't believe her. To be fair, she never fully believed herself.

"So," Exene said, as she brushed the crumbs off her jeans. "What do you think?"

"About what?" Boo's voice hadn't changed, still crisp and dusky. They used to sneak up to the rooftops, stare out at the wooded campus surrounded by the bright sparks of the city, watching giant aero-cnidarians, air-born jelly fish, drift in glowing strands overhead. Far underneath the floating creatures, they drank and dreamed and made love, adding their own noises to the ocean of night.

"Very funny," Exene sighed. Across the edge of the distant shore, a series of flashing red lights slid, like rubies running down the neck of a corpse. Police cars, perhaps escorting some mysterious dignitary to or from the spaceport. "She's a fruit roll-up. And she whispers. All the time now—bird calls, the ends of sentences. She's a wind chime with playback."

Boo stared at her, his brow furrowed. "Maybe you should sew bells on her and hang her in your window."

"Fuck you, Boo, this is serious. If anyone hears her, or finds her—" Exene shivered and pulled her scarf tighter around her neck. "I'm so screwed. I should have burned it. But the body is—I couldn't get rid of it. I've never seen anything like it. It's not normal."

"Not normal." Boo smiled. His lips were the same rich shade of red as the winking lights on the shore. "And that made you think of me."

"That's not fair."

"Well." Boo inspected the weave of his skirt. "I wouldn't know about fair, now, would I?"

Exene didn't take the bait. "I know this sounds insane, but I think she's still alive. I just don't know *how* she could be. I have no way to prove it."

"I thought this was your thing. Death and transmutation and the mysteries of the flesh?"

"Please. I'm not a doctor, I'm barely in pre-med. I am so in over my head."

"Sneak it into a lab, leave it there. Let some professor with a hard-on for paper dolls find it."

"Don't be gross. I don't want her cut up or experimented on. That's just cruel."

"As opposed to leaving her hanging in a garment bag all day long, and a bathrobe hook all night?"

"If they find the body, they'll hand it over to campus police."

"People go missing all the time, accidentally and on purpose. Especially on campus. No one cares."

From underneath the continual hum of traffic and machines, a sonorous gong sounded, followed by another that echoed over the bay. Exene stood up and walked to the edge of the ruins, letting waves splash at her boots as she watched.

"An ocean cult," Boo said, fumbling in his backpack. "Shit, I don't have my camera."

At the far left curve of waterfront, the front end of a flotilla of junks and boats appeared. Several of the junks were trailing balloons—wind-filled figures of round and puffy sea creatures that rose in the air like mini-dirigibles. One boat sailed a balloon man, a cream-colored stick figure whose fabric body undulated and shimmied as if dancing across the buildings lining the shore. Around them, air jellies hovered like gossamer flowers, unaware they were courting versions of themselves that could never love them in return.

The gong sang out again, and Exene heard the far-off cry of human voices, chanting to their unseen water god as they steered their way to the open ocean, never to return.

"We should get back," Exene said. "It'll be sunset soon. This place gets creepy after dark."

"You loved it here during the summer."

"Everything's easy to love in the summer. It's winter now."

Boo laughed, and shook his head. Exene's cheeks burned. "You're a real piece of work, Exene," he said, as he threw his sandwich crust onto the rocks for the waiting gulls. "I don't hear from you for six whole months; and then this. No apology, no 'how are you doing— or stupid me, I thought for a split second you might have— No, it's just blah blah, me me me, my problems. Except, it's *my* problem now, because I know you have the body of a dead girl stashed in your dorm room." He stood up, the wind ruffling his black curls. "Thanks, Exene. Because, you know, I just didn't have enough to worry about. Hey, at least now I know how I really have to change if I want to hold your interest."

"I'm sorry I wasted your time. I won't bother you again." Exene grabbed her bag and started back through the rubble and overgrown weeds to the road.

"Don't you want to know if my penis is gone yet?"

"It's none of my business!" she shouted back.

"No? You sucked it enough times to make it your business!"

Exene reached the edges of the cracked stone road, and began walking at a brisk pace, eager to reach the subway station before the light faded. She heard Boo catch up to her, his footfalls keeping time with hers as he trailed behind. Out on the water, the cult's flotilla disappeared into the wide curve of the bay, and the steady beat of the gongs fading into the city's perpetual ambient thrum. Exene shivered and tugged at her scarf again, little protection against the saltwater winds. She should have worn a heavier coat; she'd forgotten how much colder it was along the shore.

"Here." Boo stepped up beside her, his large eyes catching a spark of the remaining light. They stopped, and he pushed her hair back, slipping his fur ear muffs over her head.

"Thanks." Exene reached up to adjust them, and he grabbed her wrists. Slowly, gently, he moved her right hand down to below his waist, placing it firmly against his crotch. Exene felt her cheeks prickle in embarrassment, but she didn't pull her hand away. His body felt smooth beneath her palm.

"You're looking for me in the wrong place," Boo said. He placed her left hand on his chest, in the hollow between two small, new breasts. "I know nothing stays the same. But inside, there's something that does. You fell in love with what I am inside. That hasn't changed. Do you understand?"

Exene kept her hand on his heart, and moved her other up to his face. His skin was soft, like liquid glass. "You know I do. But, the way we look, how we grow and change and decay—that also makes us who we are. And it makes the people around us change, whether we want it to or not. I'm sorry."

"I know." Boo's voice caught on the words. Exene reached up to brush a stray tear from his face, and a movement beyond his shoulders caught her eyes.

"Boo, look."

From across the bay, barely skirting the white-capped waters, the large balloon man floated toward them, broken free of the flotilla. Behind him, a translucent air jelly jetted, its fragile body expanding and contracting as it rode the wake of its intended mate. As the silk cords hit the stony shoreline, the balloon shot up again, buoyed by a sudden gust, and the jelly soared in unison. Exene watched the figures move inland, over warehouses and factories, her smile fading as they grew smaller. Small as humans. Translucent as human skin.

"Some things never change," Boo said.

"Everything changes," said Exene. "And yet, everything stays the same."

The Simple Crimp Fold

Exene woke up with a start.

Laith.

She slid out of bed and tiptoed to her desk. In the moonlight, Kylie looked on in black-eyed curiosity, her mouth a portal of questions. Exene slid the campus phone book from out of a stack of papers, and flipped through the pages, her finger sliding down the names until she found him.

"What time is it—what's going on?" Boo, from the bed. She'd brought him back to her room to look at Kylie, and he'd ended up staying the night. Exene had been reluctant, but they fell asleep only spooning, and nothing more. It had been lovely. She hadn't realized how much she had missed talking to him, how well she still fit in the embrace of his arms. In *her* arms, she corrected herself. In hers.

"Sorry," Exene whispered. She dialed the number on the rotary, and waited.

"Yeah?" A sleepy male voice answered.

"It's Exene."

Silence. Then: "Oh."

"What did you mean when you said, 'I tried to unwrap her'?"

More silence.

"Did you know what was happening to her?"

"No, I—" His receiver fell, and Exene heard fumbling. He was crying, she realized with a start. Boo moved beside her, and they sat on the bed together, heads pressed close to the phone.

"*I couldn't unwrap her.* You knew," Exene said. "She wasn't attacking you, you were trying to help her. How did you know?"

"I'm sorry about the calls," Laith said. "But I didn't know what to do, and you wouldn't give her back—it's never happened like that before."

"What's never happened?"

"They walked in on us, Mal and Darin, I had to tell them something, and make them lie—they thought they were protecting me. But you have to understand—I didn't kill her, because—"

"—she's not dead."

Laith fell silent. Exene's heart twisted in her chest.

"You said this happened before. Are you like her? Is this going to happen to you, too?"

Barely-whispered: "Yeah. Maybe. Like I said, it's never happened like that before."

"This happened to other students?"

"Haven't you seen it yet?" His voice sounded so small in her night-filled room. "It's happening to all of us. You, too."

Silence filled up the lines.

Exene felt her mouth go dry. She could barely move her tongue. "Are you human?"

"Are you?"

"What does that mean?"

Exene held her breath as Laith spoke, his crackly voice sounding centuries away. "People say they adapt, but we have no idea what the word means—it's not anything we do. We're a part of this world, this ocean, and everything in it. Can't you feel it?"

Exene pressed at the pain in her chest. She thought of the great machines plowing up the mysterious skin of her homeworld, of settlers wasting away into rotting vegetable husks, black flesh scattering into the pink skies like seeds. Like carnelian colored corn. That would have been her someday, if she'd stayed. But she's here. What would happen if she removed her fingers from the hollow between her breasts? Would her cnidarian heart break free, and float away?

"We're being terraformed," Exene said.

From the door, Kylie swayed in the heat of the clanking radiator, a phosphorescent glow traveling through her gossamer skin.

"You haven't hurt her, have you?" asked Laith.

"No, of course not. Why didn't you say something that night? I would have given her to you, you know, if I'd known."

Laith blew his nose. "I don't know. I was scared. And drunk, and I couldn't get away from Mal and Darin. I didn't know how to act around all of you. Everything's still so new. You have to understand, I don't know what happens next—I don't know what to do."

Boo whispered into Exene's ear, *he's just a kid.*

"Laith, I know it's the middle of the night, but why don't you come on over? I think I know how to help you and Kylie both." *Do you mind*, she mouthed to Boo, who nodded *no* as she slipped from the bed. "Yeah, I'll give you directions. Yeah, get a paper and pen."

Boo opened a window pane, and night air bled through the warm room, scented with the salt and metallic tang of city and sea. She turned back and grabbed her clothes from the floor—Exene watched as Boo looked up, pupils black and wide. Sparks of green floated through them, phosphorescent dots that flared like fireflies.

"You were born on this planet, weren't you?" Exene said.

Boo only stared down, an enigmatic smile at her lips.

. . . *weren't you.*

"When you said you were transitioning, I thought, I just assumed you meant surgery, but you meant—"

Boo shrugged. "I just changed. I just—became myself, finally."

. . . myself, finally.

The Valley Fold

Exene wrote a letter to her homeworld, gave it a single fold, then let it float into the O of her trash can, leaving the silver courier packet empty on the desk. No one there remembered her, anymore. She took the photo of her parents and pressed it to the window, so they could see what she saw, see the living city spread out across the ocean's curve like a galaxy of starfish sailing through the night, and forgive her. It wasn't just the best she could do. It was the best she could do.

The Mountain Fold

Morning dawned clear and dry, with pale blue sky overhead, and a spring foehn wind that set trees rattling down to their roots and flower petals flying—she'd been right. What a difference two months made. Yet in two months more, the summer heat would blast all this frail beauty away. Nothing stayed the same here very long. Exene dressed warm, and packed her bag carefully. She glanced at the back of the door before opening it, ran her hands over the clamps of the hanger. It swayed at her touch, clacking against the wood. The sound just wasn't the same.

Boo waited in the downstairs lobby, his hand clasped tight in Laith's grasp. Exene had seen the signs, weeks ago. She was glad for their newly-found happiness, although slivers of regret still pricked at her heart. In silence they filed through a maze of burnt orange furniture and lounging students, and out the glass doors into the quiet campus, and then past thick stone gates into the chaos of the day. Boo consulted the subway map, and they made their way through thick traffic and crowds to the nearest stop, descending underground and onto the 14 line. "It'll take at least three hours to get there, maybe more with all the stops," Boo had warned, but Exene had been insistent, and Laith agreed.

After ninety minutes, the train switched from underground to elevated: Exene pressed her face against the scratched glass panes, Kylie heavy against her back. She'd never been this far inside the city—it was inland, far past the industrial sections and suburban sprawl. It was country. Low buildings and wide spaces instead of the claustrophobic crush of skyscrapers, with fields and wood-ringed clearings. There were real houses here, real roads, and endless sky— this floating, feral city was a continent, she realized, its vastness a place she could free herself in, not be trapped by. Something in her heart broke free, and soared. It was as if she were going home, all the centuries scrubbing themselves away.

Another hour of travel took them to a series of foothills, craggy mounds dotted with jagged pylons and gnarled trees. They walked from the empty station on a gravel and dirt road that wound its way up through pitted wrought-iron gates, and into a cemetery that covered an entire hill—one of the oldest in the city, long abandoned. "Up there," Exene pointed, as the winds whipped her hair into a frenzied dance. They made their way over paths and lawns choked with weeds, until they reached the apex. Exene slipped the bag from her back, and handed it to Boo, who held it out to Laith, as she turned in a circle.

From all points below, the city stretched out and away, so far that its tips were lost in mist and haze. Dirigibles and copters caught the light as they flew back and forth around the slivers of glass and steel—it all seemed so calm from here, so manageable. Exene held up her fingers, pinching them to pretend she held each building in her grasp. The wind up here was only itself, carrying no scent of ocean or manmade sound.

"Exene."

She lowered her hands and turned to watch Laith unfurl Kylie from the bag. Exene had rolled her up again last night, this time handling the fragile skin with all the gentle respect due a metamorphosing being. Boo and Laith held Kylie's body still, as Exene threaded a silk cord around her waist, careful to knot the end just so.

"You're sure you know what you're doing?"

"Yep," Exene said to Boo. "I used to do this all the time back home, all the kids did. I haven't forgotten."

They waited. Below, the city glinted in the sun. The wind gusted, a long hard wave that knocked the leaves in roaring pinwheels from the trees; and Exene began to run, the end of the cord wrapped tight around her fist. And when she shouted *now*, Boo and Laith let go. Exene looked back as she ran, watching the silk cord rise, watching Kylie rise. The girl caught the air, her papery skin inflating, plumping out. Laith and Boo caught up to her, watching as Exene guided Kylie through the currents, sending her higher and higher into the skies.

"I hope that's me someday," Laith said. "I hope she's not lonely till then. What if she gets lost, or leaves?"

Kylie looked down at them from below—for the first time in months, her toothless mouth was closed, but her lips seemed to be remembering what it was to smile. Exene returned the smile as she watched Kylie's limbs move with and against the currents. Testing the waves, so to speak, before she took off on her own.

"I'm sure you'll find her again, wherever she goes."

"I just don't want to be alone. I mean, I don't want to be the only one. You know?"

Exene glanced at Boo.

"No one does," she said.

Above them, spring wind rushed through Kylie's openings, playing the hollowed flesh like a flute as it gushed from her mouth. She sang—high, pure notes that floated through the air like a nightingale's call. Exene felt Boo's hand steal into hers, her fingers warm and strong.

"Do you think they'll ever be a time when we understand each other?" Laith asked. "When all of us truly belong?"

"Does it matter?" Exene replied. She gave the cord two quick tugs, and it spun down to the ground in silky spirals. Kylie floated away, singing as she soared.

Philomela in Seven Movements

Natalia Theodoridou

On Mondays, she is a bird.
She feeds him her egg, sunny side up and runny.
"It's yummy," he says. "You should make this more often."

On Tuesdays, she is a tree.
Trees speak. Their stories have no verbs. They say, over and over:
"My leaves. My trunk. The air. The birds. The light. The earth. My
    leaves. My leaves. My leaves."

On Wednesdays, her smile is stuck to the back of her head.
She walks around scaring people.

On Thursdays, she stays in
with a bad case of wandering womb.

On Fridays, her skirt floats around her
like a mournful sail in the Aegean.
"Who died?" he teases.

On Saturdays, she is a continent.
"Only you and I here, my love," she says. "Your axe and my wound.
My love, my love."

On Sundays, she forgets her name.
She thinks she's a bird,
and sings.

Mortar/Pestle

Jane Yolen

Baba Yaga has never learned to drive a car
though she travels many miles each day,
sailing in her granite mortar, steered by a pestle.
The thing smells of crushed garlic, borscht,
dark Turkish cigarettes, kvass,
a Russian stew of bad habits, and tall tales.

No one sees her of course. She doesn't exist
unless you count bad dreams. Yet still she flies,
the friendly and unfriendly skies,
across tundra, taiga, major highways,
avoiding traffic jams, roundabouts,
only bothering the occasional helicopter
or low-flying private planes.

Now and then, aliens are reported,
or the government says she's a weather balloon,
or sometimes an incoming storm.
But that blip of unknown origin means
she's off to the grocery store or the bingo parlor,
mahjong game, or bowling alley again.
Or maybe the latest Wolverine movie—
she sure loves her Hugh Jackman,
though she says his teeth are too white, too even,
wonders how he can eat with those choppers,
gnashes her own.

When she gets going nothing,
nothing stands in her way.

Sing the Crumbling City

C.S. MacCath

The Völva steps through the universe fissure singing. One black-heeled pump hammers the nail of the rhythm down, down, down; the other, in the sucking hole of the void, pins the real to the road for the rest of the band. The brown halo of her natural hair bobs as her head sways, and the vibrato of her voice is a suture of the ancient city to itself over the spacetime wound. The Protégé edges around her onto broken cobblestones. Calluses bleed on the strings of his screaming guitar. Platinum hair paints the blood across a white sleeve and whips in the high wind with a toss of his head. He sings the counter-melody with a full and earnest mouth, ready to carry the song alone if his mentor succumbs. Behind them both, the Conservator is a paradox of here and not-here, bass pounding from an interstitial place, light from a faraway sanctuary golden against the dead, gray sky. It shines on the others while a low-octave line of music tethers them to safety, to home. Together, they are the Voice of What Should Have Been, of a great city that once rose like an evening star over the many worlds of humankind, of a universe broken on the knee of a bully's ambition.

The flesh eyes of the Völva fix upon the frozen tower clock in the Gammel Quarter, but her spirit eyes watch the seconds hand tick above a bustle of shoppers in the Spacetime of Her Awakening. *Evie will have heard us there first*, she thinks, holding a seventh note like a scalpel raised, *if the message we play her is powerful enough*. The seventh resolves, the scalpel descends and the Völva splits the veil between *now* and *then*:

> "What. We who raise the warning cry—
> summon the sleight of your seiðr-kenning!
> Mímir's well, might of the Maddener beckons;
> drink and know Níðhöggr gnaws at the root."

Evie blinks at the ticking tower clock behind a glare of summer sunlight, blinks again and turns toward peculiar music. Mist from a nearby fountain dampens her cheek. Children plash in the water. There, in front of the bakery, a veil parts the world, leaches color from blossomy trees and storefront displays, supplants it with twilight. A parcel slips from her fingers and lands with a crash on the cobblestones. A mother walks by with a double stroller, frowns at her, keeps walking. An old man with a cane totters behind.

"They don't see it." The words are a sub-vocal murmur. Her teeth clench around a cherry lozenge, crushing it. A woman fades in from the gray; coffee-skinned, navy dress suit, spiky heels and sings beside a pale guitarist with sapphires for eyes. Behind them, the belly-deep sound of a bass thrums from a body-shaped shimmer of yellow light. Their music is a clap of thunder before a storm, the wail of a young widow, birdsong. A pair of lovers amble past, arm-locked. "They don't hear it either." Evie swallows a shard of lozenge, unmelted in her dry mouth, and falls to her knees, shaking.

> "Your universe is yielding to its teeth.
> The lore-lies in your learned father's mouth—
> obscure the spacetime schism he begets.
> Urðarbrunnr echoes with the ego of a tyrant."

The Völva's voice softens as she watches Evie stand. Blond curls float about her face in a gust of wind and stick to tear-stained cheeks dotted with freckles. She is small, plain and forgettable, a creature accustomed to flinching, who flees as if she is always running away. Her dress billows at the hem like a flag of surrender.

A silvery jitter joins the veil at the split, separates a living past from a dying present. Here-now, the city is bleak and forbidding, its riven Gammel Quarter a foyer that opens to entropy. In the distance, a cluster of skyscrapers crumble inside a plexus of fragmented highways, and a pair of space elevators hang unconnected from moons in the sky. Universe fissures, ragged and wide, gape like ravenous grendels in the landscape.

The Conservator retreats into the void, and the Protégé follows, fingering a steady bridge between verses. The Völva crosses it with him, through the awful nothingness to the Spacetime of Her Liberation. Shattered solar panels clutter the wreck of the Capitol Square in the place where Evie's father will have told of the thing he built. Concrete dust rises in a cloud and coats the tongue. The Völva swallows, gathers power into her throat and sounds a note so high it pierces time:

> "His cruelty to the cosmos cries for reckoning;
> weaver of wyrd, we await you at the loom.
> Heal what the heart's foe harrowed in his home,
> and sing of what we show you, Sverrir's daughter."

Sverrir's daughter. Evie's body quakes with adrenaline, and her bowels ache with a sudden need to evacuate. Snow flurries pass through a veil overlaid on the Walk of Worlds, where the flags of colony planets snap at the wintry sky. Raucous music rings in the square, but as before, in the summer, the crowd behind her is deaf to it. *They're singing to me.*

"You're singing to me," she says aloud. A man with a video camera turns in response, arches an eyebrow, turns away. The woman beside him points a microphone at the capitol steps.

Across the gulf between the city and the city, a yellow light flickers. A guitar string breaks. The black-eyed singer chokes and fills her lungs.

Atop the steps, Evie's father signals for silence. Watery daylight gleams on the signet ring he never removes, encoded to lock—among other things—her bedroom window and door. Even from several feet away, the spice of his aftershave is strong; a reminder of masculine sweat, a stick in a fist, the bruises under her jumper and coat. He smiles around perfect teeth, fingers a blond forelock into place and begins to speak.

"Quantum mechanics tells us that after two particles separate, whatever happens to one is mirrored in the other." His index fingers connect, point and diverge, twirling in turn to illustrate his explanation. "For many hundreds of years, we've used this principle of physics to communicate with our sister colonies." He pauses, charms with a knowing smile. "Beginning in the summer, we'll use it to visit them."

"Soon, star-farers will assail the astral cloth—"

Spittle flies from the singer's mouth. Sweat cakes dust on the ancient recording device in her palm. She holds it forth like a talisman, and footage appears of travelers passing through opaline conduits over many millennia.

Evie slides between the cameraman and reporter to watch. Her gaze flits to her father and back again.

Sverrir waits for a babble of questions to ebb. Snow collects on the sleeves of his coat. He brushes it off and sweeps an arm across the horizon. "A second age of exploration is upon us, limited only by the boundaries of the universe!"

"—weakening the warp and weft until it sunders."

The conduits darken and sag. Others open, but these are the maws of monsters that feed upon the city, the planet and its moons, the colony worlds and all of the cosmos.

Evie's bruises ache with dread. She scowls at the man who raised them. *You ruin everything you touch.*

Sverrir frowns at her sudden fire, a private expression replete with terrible promise, and loses command of the crowd. Questions trickle into the silence again. "It's absolutely safe," he answers one. "I've traveled through it myself," he answers another. "There is no danger whatsoever."

"Who inflicts upon the future a fate well-known to him—"

A liquid quickening of sound brings the band back into focus. The guitarist is pouring his talent into a solo, high and desperate. Blood spatter dries on the fretboard, the strings, the backs of his hands.

He knows? Evie presses a fist to frozen lips. A memory replies, of an accident at the beta site. And another, of a whitewash painted over the many who died. *Of course he does.*

A nearby street vendor lays a row of sausages on a grill. Fat sizzles and pops under the din of guitar and discussion. Sverrir raises his voice with subtle distaste, as if the act of shouting were the province of lesser men. "Our sister colonies are completing construction now. In the summer, when you're able to travel between them, you'll see for yourselves what a wonder we've built for you!"

"—lies below the earth when the long night comes."

The shimmer of yellow light dims to black. A being emerges from the darkness; eyes wholly amber in a face too wide, skin a mottled crimson and bronze. Long fingers dance over an elegant bass guitar strapped to a body that towers over the others. The slack set of its angular jaw is unreadable, but its companions are frightened now, and the music rattles with it.

Evie steps into the center of the square, toward the band only she can see, and begins to scream. The crowd quiets as she points a shaking finger at her father, and the torrent of sound evolves into a litany of his sins. Sverrir's quick allegation of schizophrenia seethes with pity. Paramedics close in from the edge of the crowd. The cameraman and reporter intervene to hold them off, and the veil shuts as Evie's tongue sharpens into a scourge.

Bone and cartilage crackle as the Protégé folds his hands, weeping with pain. The Völva disgorges a clot of gritty mucus and gathers him into her arms. They cannot travel the fissures now; the tether is broken. The Conservator is livid with failure; eyes and skin purpling like contusions, chemosignals reeking of sulfur and sorrow. So they walk the length of the city to the conduit hub, where Evie will have gone if she escaped the Capitol Square. The desolate boroughs along the way are pocked with paths to the void, and the Conservator plays when it passes them, teasing tendrils of light from the dark that never connect with the instrument calling them forth.

The Spacetime of Her Power sits on the shore of an empty ocean bed. A jigsaw puzzle missing pieces of building and beach, it remembers the sea like a departed wife, in the shimmer of her salt on its rusting girders and rising stones. If the Völva can sing now at all, it will be over a roar of wind that pulls from every direction into emptiness. They do not dare to approach, so the Voice of What Should Have Been sets up in the wreck of the street and steels itself to play over a ribbon cutting and speeches. The Conservator lays down a riff that is only a series of notes. The Protégé fills it in with a bar of triplets. The Völva opens her throat and hopes.

"Seiðkona! Sing the crumbling city to itself.
Foretell the tale to travelers and witnesses.

Remake the march of days; mend the starry plain,
and bring oblivion to the blight Skuld forgot."

In the city that was, a high tide bathes a half-moon beach in
brine and sprays the glass-fronted conduit hub that frames it. Three
colossal screens rise from a stage in front of the building, blocking
the midsummer sun. Sverrir steps to a shaded podium, taps the mi-
crophone and scans the upturned faces of reporters and travelers,
perhaps for his missing daughter.

Evie's lips part in a lipstick sneer. Kohl-painted eyes fix on the
center image of her father's distant face. Between them, a murmur-
ing multitude waits behind a red velvet rope that separates the rabble
from the press and the fortunate few who will cross to the colonies
today. She lifts a protest placard into the air. A handful of angry new
friends do the same. Sverrir opens his mouth to speak, and the mul-
titude quiets.

Faint music makes her turn and scan the street. In dreams, the
singer there is a goddess of vengeance, the handsome guitarist a lover
and the alien bassist a creature of light and strangeness. But in reality
they are only pitiful people, stretched to the edges of their endurance,
and the landscape they inhabit is only a watermark on the world.

Sing the crumbling city to itself. Poetry, like memory, permeates
her mind, triggers epiphany. *Foretell the tale to travelers and witnesses.*
She looks forward into the faces of the musicians, back at the giant
images of the man about to speak and understands her place between
them, at the center of all things. *Remake the march of days; mend the
starry plain.* Power, raw and sudden, rises in her throat. *Bring oblivion
to the blight Skuld forgot.* She reaches up, finds the whistle register at
the top of her vocal range and hangs upon it like a limber acrobat
without a net.

A gust of wind snatches the placard away. The watermark land-
scape resolves, and music begins to pour through the veil. The rabble
turn like a herd on the hoof, startled by this intrusion of noise. Evie's
penetrating tone resolves into song:

"Look, and see the future I have seen—"

Beyond the red velvet rope, the fortunate few stir, their attention
divided. Sverrir sputters, and the lines around his mouth are mag-

nified on the screens behind him. The Völva watches them harden from across a chasm of centuries, her counterpoint a threnody implacable as the death it proclaims.

"Bruises on the blazing bodies of the stars!"

Shouldered cameras turn from the stage, part the crowd, advance. Evie follows a trill of lightning triplets on the guitar, and for a moment she and the Protégé are a single instrument, keening.

"—the city and the colonies crushed by a lie—"

The Conservator's neck flares in a shimmer of ridges, and the rumble of its chord progression raises the key a third. Beside it, the Völva cedes the center of attention, falls in behind Evie and matches the sway of her hips.

"Worlds once blooming are withered and gray!"

Sverrir peers at the band, at the veil, recognizes his daughter and leaps onto the sand like a predatory cat. Evie bares her teeth in a battle grin, and her black boot hammers the nail of the rhythm down, down, down.

"—told by a monster who murders with his mind—"

Three new video feeds appear above the stage; a collage of audiences across the capitol and colonies. *They are all watching now*, the Völva thinks, her voice rising in the crescendo that precedes a final fall.

"The artifacts of intellect everywhere undone,"

Evie's father rushes toward the girl who dares to defy him, skids to a stop, grips her denim jacket in a fist, rears back with the other. Shouts of protest rise from the rabble, but the creature accustomed to flinching fills her lungs instead and wields the song like a sonic weapon.

"—and doesn't care if he leaves your kids to die!"

Strong men separate the tyrant from his daughter, who shines like a waxing moon in the wake of her words. The Protégé and the Conservator complete the coda together, and then the Völva offers a closing a cappella phrase to the past.

"and the silence of sentience stolen by greed."

Black-clad police come to take Sverrir away and contain the crush of people pushing out into the street. Above the stage, the center screen is filled with Evie's face tilted up at itself in wonderment. Billions of voices rise on either side from every world in witness. "Seiðkona!" they chant like a prayer. "Seiðkona!"

She turns toward the band, touches fingers to her lips and blows a girlish kiss across time. The Protégé sweeps a shaking hand into the air and catches it to press against his heart. Behind him, the crumbling city evanesces in a fog of unmaking; from frozen tower clocks to rusting girders and rising stones. Near the shore of an empty ocean bed, at the edge of a broken universe, the Voice of What Should Have Been bows at the waist with a weary flourish and fades, fades with the rest until it is gone.

Delirious Mythology

About the Contributors

Saira Ali grew up in the deep south of the United States and has still not acclimatized to New England winters. Saira is both an engineer and a poet, and rejects false dichotomies in all forms. Her work has also appeared in *Strange Horizons, Stone Telling*, and *The 2015 Rhysling Anthology*, and will appear in the forthcoming anthology *Angels of the Meanwhile* edited by Alexandra Erin.

Born in the year of Halley's Comet, **Michele Bannister** spends her days chasing yesterday's light. She currently lives in British Columbia. Her poetry has appeared in *Strange Horizons, Stone Telling, Goblin Fruit*, and other venues, and in the *Here, We Cross* anthology (2012).

Alicia Cole lives with a tarot-reading familiar and a passel of animal babies. She's the co-founder of Priestess & Hierophant Press, a working occultist, and a bit of a hermit. Unless she's at The Yacht Club. Or Java Lords, both in Atlanta's Little Five Points. A Best-of-the-Net Finalist and Dwarf Stars Nominee, she's her work has appeared or is forthcoming in *Darkly Told, Torn Pages Anthology, Rainbow Rumpus, The Dawntreader*, and *The Martian Wave*.

Galen Dara likes monsters, mystics, and dead things. She has created art for *Uncanny Magazine*, 47North publishing, Skyscape Publishing, Fantasy Flight Games, Tyche Books, *Fireside Magazine, Lightspeed, Lackington's*, and Resurrection House. She has been nominated for the Hugo, the World Fantasy Award, and the Chesley Award. When Galen is not working on a project you can find her on the edge of the Sonoran Desert, climbing mountains and hanging out with a loving assortment of human and animal companions. Her website is www.galendara.com and you can follow her on twitter at @galendara.

Jeannine Hall Gailey recently served as the second Poet Laureate of Redmond, Washington. She is the author of four books of poetry: *Becoming the Villainess, She Returns to the Floating World, Unexplained Fevers* and *The Robot Scientist's Daughter*, out in spring 2015 from Mayapple Press. Her work has been featured on NPR's *The Writer's Almanac, Verse Daily*, and in *The Best Horror of the Year Vol. 6*. Her poems have appeared in *The American Poetry Review, The Iowa Review* and *Prairie Schooner*. Her website is www.webbish6.com.

Gwynne Garfinkle lives in Los Angeles. Her poetry and fiction have appeared in numerous publications, including *Strange Horizons, Interfictions, Apex Magazine, Postscripts to Darkness,* and *The Mammoth Book of Dieselpunk*. For more about her work, visit her website, gwynnegarfinkle.com.

Brady Golden's work has recently appeared in *Kaleidotrope, DarkFuse Vol. 2*, and on the podcast *Pseudopod*. He currently lives in Oakland, California with his wife, daughter, and an indeterminate amount of cats.

Adam Howe is a British writer of fiction and screenplays. Writing as Garrett Addams, his short story Jumper was chosen by Stephen King as the winner of the *On Writing* contest, and published in the paperback/Kindle versions of King's book. His fiction has appeared in places like *Nightmare Magazine, Thuglit, Horror Library 5* and *One Buck Horror*. His novella collections, *Black Cat Mojo* and *Die Dog Or Eat The Hatchet*, are available now from Comet Press. His novella *Gator Bait* is available as an eBook single. He is currently writing his first novel, *One Tough Bastard*. Tweet him at @Adam_G_Howe.

John Philip Johnson has just come out with a collection of graphic poetry, *Stairs Appear in a Hole Outside of Town,* illustrated by Marvel Comics legend Bob Hall and others. It's a comic book, and a sample can be found at http://www.rattle.com/poetry/tag/graphic-poetry/. He has work recently published or forthcoming from *Rattle, Strange Horizons, Apex Magazine, Niteblade, Daily Science Fiction* and Ted Kooser's newspaper column, "American Life in Poetry." He lives in Lincoln, Nebraska, with his wife and three or four of their five children. John, and the comic book, can be reached through his website, www.johnphilipjohnson.com.

Jamie Killen's work has appeared or is forthcoming in *Electric Velocipede*, *Scheherezade's Bequest*, *Space and Time*, and anthologies *Read by Dawn* volumes II and III and *Heiresses of Russ 2013*. She lives in Arizona with a Dalek. Her website is https://jamieskillen.wordpress.com/.

Swapna Kishore lives in India and writes fiction and non-fiction. Her speculative fiction has appeared in *Nature* (*Futures*), *Fantasy Magazine*, *Strange Horizons*, *Ideomancer*, *Sybil's Garage No. 7*, *Warrior Wisewoman 3*, *Breaking the Bow*, *Apex Book of World SF* (Volume 3), and various other publications and anthologies. She has published books on software engineering and process management, including a business novel. She also blogs about dementia care in India and creates online resources for dementia caregivers in English and Hindi. Her website is at swapnawrites.com.

Margo Lanagan's first published work was poetry, in small Australian literary magazines in the 1980s. She's since carved out a career as a speculative fiction and young-adult author, writing novels and short stories. The occasional poem still happens along.

Geoffrey A. Landis is a writer, a poet, and a scientist. He has won the Hugo and Nebula awards for best science fiction, and the Rhysling award for best poem. His poetry chapbooks include *Iron Angels* (vanZeno, 2009) and *The Book of Whimsy* (NightBallet, 2015). He is also the author of the novel *Mars Crossing* and the story collection *Impact Parameter (and Other Quantum Realities)*. He was recently named the recipient of the 2014 Robert A. Heinlein Award "bestowed for outstanding published works in science fiction and technical writings that inspire the human exploration of space." More information can be found at his web page, http://www.geoffreylandis.com/.

Nathaniel Lee lives and works less than willingly in North Carolina with his spouse and son. His fiction appears in *Beneath Ceaseless Skies*, *Ideomancer*, and *Daily Science Fiction*, as well as dozens of other online and print venues. He also works as the assistant/managing editor for *Escape Pod* and the *Drabblecast*, respectively.

Rose Lemberg was born in Ukraine, and lived in subarctic Russia and Israel before immigrating to the US, where she works as a professor of Nostalgic and Marginal studies. Rose's prose and poetry have appeared in *Strange Horizons*, *Apex*, *Beneath Ceaseless Skies*, *Unlikely Story*, *Interfictions*, and other venues. She edits *Stone Telling* with Shweta Narayan, and is preparing to release her first anthology of fiction-like writing, *An Alphabet of Embers*. Rose can be found at roselemberg.net, and on Twitter as @roselemberg.

Livia Llewellyn is a writer of dark fantasy, horror and erotica. Her fiction has appeared in numerous magazines and anthologies, including *Subterranean*, *Nightmare Magazine*, and *Postscripts*, and her short story collection *Engines of Desire: Tales of Love & Other Horrors* was nominated for the Shirley Jackson Award for Best Collection. You can find her online at liviallewellyn.com.

Valya Dudycz Lupescu is the author of *The Silence of Trees* and founding editor of *Conclave: A Journal of Character*. Valya's next book, *Geek Parenting*, co-authored with Stephen H. Segal, will be out in April 2016 (Quirk Books). Valya's poetry and prose have been published in *Kenyon Review Online*, *Strange Horizons*, *Danse Macabre*, *Fickle Muses, Abyss & Apex*, *The Pedestal Magazine, Gone Long*, and other places. Since earning her MFA in writing from the School of the Art Institute of Chicago, Valya has worked as a college professor, obituary writer, content manager, goth cocktail waitress, and co-producer of an independent feature film. Her first comic book, *Sticks & Bones*, created with artist Madeline C. Matz, was successfully crowdfunded via Kickstarter. You can read more on her website, www.vdlupescu.com, and follow her on Twitter @Valya.

C.S. MacCath is a writer of fiction, non-fiction and poetry whose work has appeared in *Strange Horizons*, *Clockwork Phoenix: Tales of Beauty and Strangeness*, *Mythic Delirium* and other publications. Her poetry has been nominated twice for the Rhysling Award, while her fiction has been nominated for the Pushcart Prize and shortlisted for the Washington Science Fiction Association Small Press Award. You can find her online at csmaccath.com.

Alex Dally MacFarlane is a writer, editor and historian. When not translating from Classical Armenian or researching narrative maps in the legendary traditions of Alexander III of Macedon, Alex writes stories, found in *Clarkesworld Magazine*, *Phantasm Japan*, *Solaris Rising 3*, *Gigantic Worlds* and *The Year's Best Science Fiction & Fantasy: 2014*. Alex is the editor of *Aliens: Recent Encounters* (2013) and *The Mammoth Book of SF Stories by Women* (2014), and in 2015 joined Sofia Samatar as co-editor of non-fiction and poetry for *Interfictions Online*. "Otter Script" belongs to a project of poetry about history and space, past and future, from which other poems have been published in *Other Countries: Contemporary Poets Rewiring History*, *Stone Telling*, *Strange Horizons* and *Bahamut*. Follow @foxvertebrae on Twitter for more.

Lynette Mejía writes science fiction, fantasy, and horror prose and poetry from the middle of a deep, dark forest in the wilds of southern Louisiana. Her work has been nominated for the Rhysling Award and the Million Writers Award. You can find her online at www.lynettemejia.com.

Virginia M. Mohlere was born on one solstice, and her sister was born on the other. Her chronic writing disorder stems from early childhood. She lives in the swamps of Houston and writes with a fountain pen that is extinct in the wild. Her work has been seen in *Cabinet des Fées*, *Jabberwocky*, *Lakeside Circus*, *Goblin Fruit*, *Strange Horizons*, and *MungBeing*.

Sunny Moraine's short fiction has appeared in *Clarkesworld*, *Strange Horizons*, *Nightmare*, and *Long Hidden: Speculative Fiction from the Margins of History*, among other places. They are also responsible for the novels *Line and Orbit* (cowritten with Lisa Soem) and the *Casting the Bones* trilogy, as well as *A Brief History of the Future: collected essays*. In addition to authoring, Sunny is a doctoral candidate in sociology and a sometimes college instructor; that last may or may not have been a good move on the part of their department. They unfortunately live just outside Washington, D.C., in a creepy house with two cats and a very long-suffering husband.

Kristine Ong Muslim is the author of *We Bury the Landscape* (Queen's Ferry Press, 2012), *Grim Series* (Popcorn Press, 2012), and *A Roomful of Machines* (ELJ Publications, 2015), as well as three forthcoming books—the short story collection *Age of Blight* (Unnamed Press, 2016) and poetry collections *Lifeboat* and *Black Arcadia*, both of which will come out from university presses in the Philippines. Her poems and short stories have appeared widely in numerous publications, including a previous issue of *Mythic Delirium*. She lives in a small farming town in the Philippines and serves as poetry editor of *LONTAR: The Journal of Southeast Asian Speculative Fiction*, a literary journal published by Epigram Books in Singapore.

Dominik Parisien is an editor, poet, and writer who lives in Toronto. He is the co-editor, along with Navah Wolfe, of several upcoming anthologies for Saga Press, and the editor of *Clockwork Canada* (Exile Editions). His fiction and poetry have appeared in *Uncanny Magazine, Strange Horizons, Shock Totem, Ideomancer, Lackington's, Imaginarium 2013: The Best Canadian Speculative Writing*, and other venues. You can find him online at https://dominikparisien.wordpress.com/ and @domparisien on twitter.

Jessy Randall's poems, stories, and other things have appeared in *Asimov's, Lady Churchill's Rosebud Wristlet*, and *McSweeney's*. She is the curator of special collections at Colorado College, and her website is http://personalwebs.coloradocollege.edu/~jrandall/.

Wendy Rathbone has sold over 500 poems, as well as short stories. Her most recent short story appears in *A Darke Phantastique*. Her most recent poetry book, *Turn Left at November*, came out in 2015 from Eldritch Press. She has poetry upcoming in *Asimov's Science Fiction*. She is also the author of the science fiction novels *Pale Zenith* and *Letters to an Android*, the latter of which contains haiku. Her vampire novel, *Lace*, is just out, as well as a hot and heavy space opera gay romance, *Scoundrel*. She blogs at: http://wendyrathbone.blogspot.com/.

Sonya Taaffe's short fiction and poetry can be found in the collections *Ghost Signs* (Aqueduct Press), *A Mayse-Bikhl* (Papaveria Press), *Postcards from the Province of Hyphens* (Prime Books), and *Singing Innocence and Experience* (Prime Books), and in various anthologies including *The Humanity of Monsters*, *Genius Loci: Tales of the Spirit of Place*, and *Dreams from the Witch House: Female Voices of Lovecraftian Horror*. She is currently senior poetry editor at *Strange Horizons*; she holds master's degrees in classics from Brandeis and Yale and once named a Kuiper belt object. She lives in Somerville with her husband and two cats.

Shveta Thakrar is a writer of South Asian-flavored fantasy, social justice activist, and part-time nagini. She draws on her heritage, her experience growing up with two cultures, and her love of myth to spin stories about spider silk and shadows, magic and marauders, and courageous girls illuminated by dancing rainbow flames. Her most recent publications can be found in *The Toast*, *Faerie* magazine, and *Uncanny* magazine. When not hard at work stringing prose into delicate chains suitable for wearing out, Shveta makes things out of glitter and paper and felt, devours books, daydreams, bakes sweet treats, travels, and occasionally even practices her harp.

Natalia Theodoridou is a theatre and cultural studies scholar. Originally from Greece, she is currently based in Portsmouth, UK. Her writing has appeared in *The Kenyon Review Online*, *Clarkesworld*, *Strange Horizons*, and elsewhere. Find her at www.natalia-theodoridou.com, or say hi at @natalia_theodor on Twitter.

Sheree Renée Thomas, a native of Memphis, is the 2015 Lucille Geier Lakes Writer-in-Residence at Smith College and a 2016 Tennessee Arts Commission Fellow. A Cave Canem and NYFA Fellow, her work also appears in *Callaloo*, *storySouth*, *The New York Times*, *The Washington Post*, as well as in anthologies, including *Jalada 02: Afrofuture(s)*, *Circe's Lament*, *Memphis Noir*, *Revenge*, *The Moment of Change*, *80! Memories & Reflections on Ursula K. LeGuin*, *Mojo: Conjure Stories*, *Hurricane Blues*, *Bum Rush the Page*, *The Ringing Ear*, *MYTHIC 2*, and *So Long Been Dreaming: Postcolonial Science Fiction & Fantasy*. Sheree edited *Dark Matter: A Century of Speculative Fiction from the African Diaspora* and *Dark Matter: Reading the Bones* (2001 and 2005 World Fantasy Award). She is the author of *Shotgun Lullabies: Stories & Poems* (Aqueduct Press) and has a graphic novel forthcoming from Rosarium Publishing.

Jane Yolen, often called "the Hans Christian Andersen of America," is the author of over 350 published books, including *Owl Moon*, *The Devil's Arithmetic*, and *How Do Dinosaurs Say Goodnight?* The books range from rhymed picture books and baby board books, through middle grade fiction, poetry collections, nonfiction, and up to novels and story collections for young adults and adults. She has won two Nebulas, a World Fantasy Grand Master Award, and been named a Grand Master of sf/fantasy poetry by the Science Fiction Poetry Association. Six colleges and universities have given her honorary doctorates, and her Skylark Award—given by NESFA (the New England Science Fiction Association)—set her good coat on fire.

On weekdays, **Mike Allen** writes the arts column for the daily newspaper in Roanoke, Va. Most of the rest of his time he devotes to writing, editing, and publishing. He's the editor of *Mythic Delirium* magazine and the *Clockwork Phoenix* anthologies, and the author of novel *The Black Fire Concerto* and short story collections *Unseaming*. and *The Spider Tapestries*. He has been a Nebula Award and Shirley Jackson Award finalist, and has won three Rhysling Awards for poetry.

He receives a ton of help with all this editing from his wife, artist and horticulturalist **Anita Allen**. Her paintings and assemblages have appeared in juried art shows and on the covers of past issues of *Mythic Delirium*. Her first solo exhibition, a sculpture show full of modern monsters called *Beyond the Borders*, took place in October in the Liminal: Alternative Artspace gallery in Roanoke.

Their pets, Loki (canine) and Persephone and Pandora (feline) provide distractions. You can follow Mike's exploits as a writer at descentintolight.com, as an editor at mythicdelirium.com, and all at once on Twitter at @mythicdelirium. You can susbcribe to his newsletter at http://tinyurl.com/abattoir-memos.